Mary of Bethany
The Untold Story

By Kathy M Green

Mary of Bethany

The Untold Story

Copyright©2018 Kathy M Green

Cover design by Carli Mclean

Special Thank You....

To my husband Bill for putting up with my invasion of his office space, using my writing as an excuse for not cooking, for constantly reading chapters to him, and hiring him with no pay to be the punctuation and spelling editor-in-chief.

Thanks to Carli Maclean for the beautiful front cover. I knew she would be able to read my mind, and know just what to paint.

I am most grateful to my Beta Readers: Bill Green, Beverly Vaughn, Ladd Bennett, Wesley Sims, and especially, Dr. Emily Mofield, who gave me great insight, writing tips, as well as grammar lessons.

Thank you, Cyndi Thompson for praying me through this project, and much more. Thank you all. I could not have finished without you!

Author's Note:

This story is fiction based on Biblical facts. I have taken liberties with the time line to suit the plot. I used my imagination to make the characters come alive. Some characters in the story are fictional. I tried to make the people and places as true to the Bible times and customs as I could.

I also gave my lead character, Mary, much more freedom than the real Mary would have enjoyed during the first century in Israel.

I hope that you will see Jesus through the eyes of Mary, Martha, Lazarus, His disciples and others. Maybe you too can imagine them all as real people who could have lived and walked the earth with our Savior and Lord Jesus Christ.

I changed the Biblical story to include Mary of Bethany in the discovery of the empty tomb. According to the Bible, only Mary Jesus' mother, Salome and Mary Magdalene were there.

FORWARD

I am an old woman now but I can remember those days with Jesus as if they happened yesterday. There are others keeping records, but I have personal memories of our friendship that no one will ever know if I do not tell them.

I met Jesus when he was twelve years old. Not only did he rescue me from a very dangerous situation, he gave me a bag of seeds that absolutely changed my life. Jesus, my siblings and myself had many good times together before he ever became the great Rabbi and Messiah.

Thank goodness, my father saw to it that I had a good education, and he encouraged me to keep written accounts of my adventures, mishaps, and relationships.

Only a few special people may find my story, I hope those who do will share with me a relationship so unique and special that it changed my life forever.

I know there are caves where the Essenes are storing accounts of our days with Jesus. I have friends among them who will add my story to the other ones that Jesus' friends and followers have recorded.

CHAPTER 1

SAVED BY A STRANGER

If I had known how the story would end, I wonder if I would have been as brave, maybe a better word would be foolish, as I was on that hot dusty day long ago in Jerusalem. Fearful was not a word that too many people would use to describe me. I certainly had no fear earlier in the day. That was before I ended up in big trouble in a place I should never have been.

It was during the feast of Passover, my brother Lazarus, my sister Martha and I had gone with all the rest of our family on the short journey from our home here in Bethany to Jerusalem. We had gone there to make our sacrifice and eat the Passover meal with other members of our family.

I was about nine years old. I loved any excuse to be outside and away from my chores in the house. This longing often got me into trouble and that day was no exception.

I especially enjoyed the company of my brother Lazarus and his friends. I would hang around as close to them as I dared. Our family had celebrated the Passover meal at the home of our uncle Abner and now it was getting close to the time to return to Bethany.

The celebration was over and almost everyone was preparing to leave the city and return home.

The Passover celebration had filled the already crowded city beyond its capacity. The children ran from one group of friends and relatives to another, laughing and playing games in the dusty streets.

We were near the great temple steps. It was an awesome place to see, and a little scary too. The steps were so tall that a small child could not see the top of them.

We knew better than to run on them, but if we were quiet and stayed out of the way, we could climb up them to get a view of the whole city. From that high place, we could even see the countryside around Jerusalem.

We had been in Jerusalem for eight days and I was tired of the hot sun, the noise and even the other children. I longed for a cool place to rest. I left Lazarus, Martha, and my cousins and went in search of a quiet place and maybe a drink of water.

I climbed the temple steps. That in itself was no small feat. The steps are many and the climb is high. For a child it seemed as if I were climbing a mountain. I was certainly tired and thirsty when I reached the top. I found myself near the outer gate in the temple courtyard.

Women and girls could only go into the women's court that was just inside this gate. We could go no farther into the temple.

It was cool and quite in the women's court that day, not noisy as it was on feast day. I loved the way the temple smelled of incense and old cloth.

I only meant to stay for a minute to rest in the shade. I was afraid my mother would come looking for me. She might not let me out again if she found me

Often after a sacred feast, some of the men would linger in the city to talk about the Mosaic Law and discuss current events.

I had always loved to hear the men of my village discuss the Torah, especially the parts that described the coming of the Messiah. In fact, I often got into trouble for lingering in the synagogue at home listening to the rabbi talking when I should have been doing my chores.

This day was no different. When I got inside the Court of Women that old longing to hear the words of the prophets got the better of me.

I moved over as close as I could to the court of Israel. Women and girls were forbidden to go in to that place. I hoped that if I leaned my ear on the wall I would be able to hear what they were saying inside the room.

I could barely make out the words but the voice I heard sounded like a boy. It sounded like a boy talking to the rabbis. What kind of boy could be teaching the great rabbis of Jerusalem?

Maybe there was a place where I could hide and see for myself. No one else was there to see me. The women were all busy packing up their belongings for the trip home.

Carefully I peeked around the door to see if anyone was watching. No one was paying any attention to the door.

Everyone in the room was fascinated and listening to the boy. No one seemed to be looking in my direction. I still could not see very well from where I was. Did I dare go in there? Ignoring everything my good sense was trying to tell me, I slipped into the court of Israel and hid behind the tapestry that covered the walls.

The tapestry woven is from yarn of sheep's wool and is very thick. A small girl like me could easily hide behind it.

If I peeked out very carefully, I could see and hear everything that was happening but could jump back and hide if anyone looked in my direction.

I had never heard anyone discuss the Torah with as much knowledge as this boy did.

Surely, he was the son of a great Priest. How else did he learn so much at such a young age? He was not much older than I was.

He was not dressed in the fine clothes of a priest's son either.

In fact, he was wearing clothes of a tradesman. I heard someone call him Jesus, a common name for a boy in Judea. Who was this Jesus?

His words completely mesmerized me. I was so enraptured that I forgot where I was for a minute and then the dust from the curtains made me sneeze. I lost my balance and fell. Out I tumbled, right into the room in full view of everyone.

"Oh no!" I thought, "What will happen to me? Will I be stoned? Will they put me in prison? They will surely find my parents and Papa will never allow me out of our house again.

Oh, why was I so careless? My sister Martha warned me that girls should stay at home and mind the house. How I wish I had listened to her!"

One of the Pharisees strode across the room and grabbed me by my arm.

He was wearing a long black robe that swirled around his feet like smoke from a cauldron and he was very angry.

He was so scary looking. His beady eyes flashed and his beak-like nose reminded me of the vultures that sit on the dead branches over the tombs outside the city.

I do not know what would have happened to me if it had not been for that boy. All at once, he was by my side. "Please don't punish her. I know her and it is because of me that she is here. Punish me instead."

I could not believe my ears. He did not know me, but more than that, he offered to take my punishment. How did he know I had sneaked into the room to hear what he was saying?

A commotion at the door saved us. A guard came in with a man who said he was looking for his son.

That scary Pharisee, distracted by this new incident, told me to go find my father immediately and not leave his side until we were home. It was a miracle that he let me leave alone, but he did.

As I hurried out, I saw a woman waiting anxiously in the Court of Women where I had been. She looked so young and worried; I knew she must be the mother of the missing boy.

I could hear the conversation inside and I heard the boy say, "I'm sorry you and Mother were worried but you should have known I would be about my Father's business."

Who was that boy, I wondered? Who was the man with him if it was not the father? Where was his father? What kind of business would a boy have in the temple?

Little did I realize at the time how important the answers to those questions would be for me? Not only for me but my whole family and for all of Israel as well.

CHAPTER 2

THE TRIP HOME

I found my way back to my family as quickly as I could. I am sure my parents wondered why I was so quiet all the way home.

I truly intended to tell them what had happened in the temple, but I also knew they would be very angry with me.

I decided to wait a while and tell my mother when we were alone at home. As things turned out, I never got the opportunity to speak to her about it, but that part of the story comes later.

The boy who had helped me in the temple and his family traveled the short distance to Bethany with us. Their friends and other family members had gone on ahead to Nazareth while his parents, Mary and Joseph had turned back to look for him. Mary and Joseph had acquaintances in Bethany so they decided to visit with them before they returned to their home in Nazareth.

My brother Lazarus and Jesus liked each other right from the start. This did not surprise me much because everyone liked Lazarus. He was friendly, fun and kind too. Lazarus was the best big brother a girl could have, I loved him very much. It just seemed natural to me that everyone else would like him too.

Lazarus was sick a lot when he was a boy, even after he became a man; he was plagued with breathing problems. It seemed like every time he would be outside when it was dusty, he would have a very difficult time getting his breath. I could sometimes hear him making a wheezing sound at night when he would try to breathe. It always scared me. I guess it scared mama too because she kept him inside when it was dry and windy outside.

Jesus and Lazarus became good friends. Jesus never seemed to mind sitting inside with Lazarus when he was not feeling well. They played quiet games or talked about all sorts of boy things. They liked to sit and talk about the Holy Scriptures too. I loved to sit and listen to them when I was not outside tending my little flower garden.

Those visits with Jesus became very important later in our lives. However, I am getting ahead of myself again.

That day, on the way home from Jerusalem, was one of Lazarus' good days. He was able to breathe and seemed to be doing well outside.

I watched with envy from the shelter of my father's shadow as the boys and girls ran races and played games. The experience in the temple had made me cautious, even if my parents did not know what I had done.

I could not forget the look on the face of that Pharisee who had held on to my arm. I was afraid he might send someone to see if I had done what he had told me to do.

I am sure Father wondered why I was not out running like a wild donkey with the others, but he never said a word.

Jesus was good at all the games. He soon had a crowd of friends around him. Jesus' skin was brown from the sun; he had a quick smile and was nice to everyone, even the little children who were too young to understand the games.

Lazarus told me later that Jesus lived in Nazareth, but he had been born in Bethlehem. He was learning his father's trade.

Jesus' father, Joseph, was a very skilled carpenter and stonemason. His talents were in great demand, and Jesus often traveled with Joseph to other towns to work.

This explained the sun-tanned skin and strong arms. It is hard work building with stones. Almost all our buildings are made of stone. Some of the wealthy people use wood trim and carvings to decorate the inside rooms and Joseph was talented in all these things.

I wondered later about Jesus being born in Bethlehem. There were not many boys his age who survived the slaughter of baby boys that King Herod had ordered.

I wanted to ask my father about that. I thought I remembered something about a boy being born, a star and even some wise men.

Was there not an old man at the temple and a prophetess? Did any of this have anything to do with the boy Jesus I wondered?

I was very glad, for once, to get back to Bethany and our house. The incident at the temple seemed to shadow the whole trip home. I finally felt safe when Father shut our gate, and we went in to prepare our evening meal.

As usual, Martha was in the kitchen helping Mother, and bossing me around. I guess that is what older sisters do. Martha is the oldest child. She loves to cook, clean and work with mama.

As for me, I would rather be outside in the garden, or up in our roof top room reading. Father had taught us how to read. He even allowed Martha and myself to occasionally sit and listen to discussions in the synagogue. We had to be very quiet when that happened.

Papa said it was all right to read at home, but I should be careful not to let it get in the way

of our chores. I think he was secretly proud of me, but I also knew I had to keep quiet about it. I always resented that, and it nearly got me in trouble more than once.

Martha thinks it is weird that I like to read so much. I know she wants to be married and have babies. She is almost old enough for Father and Mother to seek a matchmaker for her.

I know she favors Nathan, the son of the olive grove owner. I have seen the looks they give each other when our families are visiting together.

Martha is going to have many offers when it is time to make a match for her. She is quite beautiful. Her hair is dark and glossy. She is always trying to tuck back the curls that often tried to peek out from under her veil. Besides that, everyone around respects our father, our mother has taught Martha well, and she will have a fine dowry.

To tell the truth, I do not care if I ever get married. Somehow, I think I will have something else to do with my life. When I pray, I often feel that God has a different plan for me. I think He wants me to do something special for Him even if I am just a girl. I ponder about this when I am alone.

That is another reason why I like to work in the garden; I can be quiet there and dream about what God might want me to do.

CHAPTER 3

FATHER'S STRANGE STORY

I did not know at the time why, but it seemed important to know more about the birth of Jesus.

I thought I remembered my parents telling the story of a baby named Jesus and some strange circumstances surrounding his birth. I cannot explain how I knew, but I felt secretly the baby might have been this same Jesus. The Jesus that had become our friend

One Sabbath after we had our midday meal, we were resting and talking together, I asked Father to tell the story of the baby and the old prophetess in the temple.

Here is the story that Father told:

There was an old widow woman who stayed in the temple all the time. She constantly fasted and prayed. Many people called her a prophetess. That woman told her story to one of our relatives and he told it to father.

The woman's name was Anna. One day she was praying for God to send the Messiah that would save Israel from our oppressors when she heard the voice of Simeon, an Israelite who also spent much time in the Temple.

Simeon was speaking to someone in the temple court.

Simeon was an old man. He said that he had asked God to allow him to live to see the promised savior.

On that particular day, Anna heard Simeon and he was speaking to someone. She saw him holding a baby boy and the old prophet had tears of joy on his face.

A young woman and a man were there with him. They had brought their first-born son to the temple for the traditional consecration and circumcision.

The mother was also presenting her sacrifice for purification. The law says women are unclean until they make a sacrifice on the eighth day after giving birth.

The man and wife were plainly dressed and only had enough money to buy two doves for the sacrifice.

They seemed to be surprised at what Simeon was saying. Anna told how Simeon had spoken a blessing over the baby. She said as soon as Simeon began to speak, she knew in her spirit that this was the promised child.

My father said Anna told anyone who would listen about this baby. Father could not remember all that Simeon had said in his blessing of the baby. He did recall that Simeon had told the mother something about a sword piercing her heart.

I thought this was very strange. How could that possibly happen to the mother and why?

I did not remember this part again until that horrible day many years later during another Passover in Jerusalem.

Father also remembered one more story. He said there were rumors that a king had been born in Bethlehem.

A very bright star had appeared in the sky over the town. The star remained there for quite some time. No one had ever seen anything like it before.

There were Shepherds who told a story about angels appearing to them in the night and they said the angels had told them the messiah had been born.

These shepherds were responsible for watching over the sacrificial lambs. These are the lambs sold during Passover for the atoning sacrifice.

The men said an angel appeared to them late one night. The angel told them to go see a baby who had been born in a stable.

Then the men said a whole bunch of angels had suddenly appeared in the sky and the night had become as bright as day.

My father said everybody knows shepherds are unreliable, and they had probably gotten drunk and just thought they had seen angels.

Nobody else in the town had seen any angels, or if they had, they were afraid to tell anyone.

Besides, who would choose a stable as a place to have a baby?

"What about the magi, Father?" I asked that day, "I heard there were rich wise men too."

Father remembered this story:

It seems that a couple of years after the time of the angels, shepherds, and a baby in a stable, some rich astronomers from the East had come to Jerusalem looking for a king that had been born. They said that a star had led them.

There was no new baby born to Herod at the time, so Herod got worried that someone was plotting to take his throne.

The rich men had said they thought the baby was in a city near Jerusalem because the star had hovered near there.

They explained that one of them had heard the name Bethlehem in a dream. These men were astronomers and seers. They would have known all about signs in the heavens. Herod knew they would have been able to discern dreams also.

Herod told them how to get to Bethlehem. Then he asked them to come back and tell him about the new king if they found him.

Herod said he wanted to pay tribute to this king also. For some reason though, no one ever saw the magi again in Jerusalem.

It was right after the visit of the magi that Herod ordered the killing of all the baby boys two years old and younger in Bethlehem and the surrounding countryside.

He figured that if all the babies were dead, his kingship would be safe. That massacre had been horrendous.

I remember my mother and her friends talking about it when they thought they were alone. It was too terrible to talk about in front of children. I am glad we lived far enough away so that Lazarus had been safe.

Later I did learn that the baby born in that cave in Bethlehem had been Jesus. I did not understand all of the events surrounding his birth until much later Jesus himself told us how he had survived the murders. The magi had indeed found his home not long after he had been born.

They had given gifts to his mother. There was a lot of gold, some frankincense, myrrh, and other valuable things. Jesus said his mother had told him she had often wondered about this marvelous visit.

A few years after the visit, Jesus' Father, Joseph, had a dream. In that dream an angel told him to get up right then and take Mary and Jesus to Egypt because their lives were in peril.

They left in the middle of the night, and only took what they could carry on a donkey. This happened just days before the soldiers came and started killing baby boys.

Mary and Joseph had stayed in Egypt for a long time. The gold from the Magi had provided for them, and helped them survive while they were away.

When they finally did come back, they moved to Nazareth because Joseph feared that Bethlehem might have still been a dangerous place for the baby. They were still living in Nazareth when we met Jesus.

CHAPTER 4

THE TRAGEDY

My mother and father were so much in love. In a way, this was unusual because traditionally, parents, with the help of a matchmaker, matched up young people for marriage. Matchmaking often left young people with little choice as to whom they would live out their lives.

That was true for Mama and Papa too, but I always wondered if Grand-papa and Grandma had not taken pity on Papa, and matched him up with a girl that he might have favored already.

However, it had happened, Mama and Papa had a wonderful relationship. Papa cherished the very ground Mama walked on. I think this made our tragedy even more painful.

I will never forget that awful day. It was hot and dry that summer. Our little garden had not provided us with as many vegetables as we needed for our family.

Thank God, Papa was a very successful merchant and always provided Mama the means to purchase extra things our family needed from the fresh market in Jerusalem.

I loved to go to the market with Mama. Vendors from all around brought their goods to the marketplace. Mama would walk there to shop. It is not far from Bethel to the big city.

If she had many items to purchase, Mama would let me come along and lead our donkey, Lucifer. We would pack our purchases on his broad strong back.

By the way, Lucifer was the perfect name for that donkey. There was no more stubborn creature in all of Judea! It was worth dealing with that ornery creature to be able to experience the excitement of market day.

I loved to tag along with Mother. She would bargain with the merchants and she always got a good deal for us. It was important to be frugal with all God had given us. Mama always warned us not to be wasteful with anything.

On that particular morning, Mama was in a hurry. She only needed a few items for a big family gathering and meal at our house. I begged to go but Mama absolutely refused.

I watched as she hurried out the gate and into the dusty road. I could see her as she approached the curve in the lane. It would be the last time I saw her alive.

That memory is as vivid today as if it had all happened only yesterday.

All of a sudden, a Roman chariot sped around the bend – He must have been on a very important mission because he was right in the middle of the road and he was going very fast.

He did not see Mama in time. As she tried to step aside, her long cloak caught in a horse's hoof. It pulled her down. The horse and chariot ran right over her. I do not know how that chariot kept from turning over.

I screamed, and ran toward her, but it was too late. She lay bleeding on the ground.

Martha heard me scream, and ran into the yard. She shoved me to the ground as she passed. She ran to Mama's side, screaming for help all the way. That soldier never even stopped.

Several men from our village came quickly, someone ran for Papa, but by the time he got to Mama, she was dead. I think she was gone the moment she hit the ground.

We buried her in a garden near our house. It was a beautiful place. The tomb had been in our family for quite some time.

Mama's accident nearly grieved us all to death. Papa never got over it. He aged 20 years in months that followed.

Thank goodness for Martha. She held everything together at home, cared for Lazarus and me, and took care of Papa as best she could.

I was very angry and sad for quite some time. I had always feared the Romans. Now my fear turned into hate. I prayed for the Messiah that God had promised to send us. I wanted him to hurry and come. I wanted him to set up his kingdom, and free us from the oppression of those awful Romans.

Father kept getting weaker all through that next year. Martha did everything she could think of to get him to eat and get out of the house. She even invited his friends to visit, but Papa was still so sad. I think seeing his friends who were married only made him grieve for Mama more.

He took to his bed about nine moons after Mama had died. He refused to get up for meals, and he did not want to see anyone.

One sad day he turned his face to the wall, and never got up again. He literally grieved himself to death.

I often felt bad for Martha. It was customary for the oldest daughter to take over the care of younger siblings if both parents died.

Martha had taken that very seriously. I know she felt it was her responsibility to care for us.

I think she resented it sometimes too. After all, she had once had hopes of marrying Nathan and having children of her own.

During that year after Papa died, Jesus was a frequent visitor in our home.

It was amazing how he would show up when one of us was having a particularly bad day.

A strange thing happened each time he came. Our sadness would not be so bad. I would feel peaceful most of the time while he was with us.

It seemed we knew in those moments, that God loved us, and He would take care of us all no matter what happened.

It was not until much later that we understood how God's peace was always present with Jesus. He eventually taught us how we too, could have that same peace. Many other things both good, and some very sad, would have to occur in our lives before that lesson became a reality.

CHAPTER 5

JESUS REFUSES TO EXPLAIN

Jesus visited out home often when we were growing up. Jesus and Lazarus spent hours talking and doing things together.

When Lazarus did not feel like going outside, he and Jesus played quite games or discussed the scriptures together. Jesus also taught Lazarus some of the building skills that Joseph and he used in their work.

Jesus even helped Lazarus build a little seat near the window in my room so I could sit and look at my herb garden.

Jesus visited often before he went away for several years – I will tell that part of the story later.

One day Jesus and Lazarus had planned to walk to Ephraim. It was not a great distance from Bethel. They were going to visit with friends there and planned to spend the night.

When Jesus got to our house that day, he found Lazarus having one of the breathing spells that he had quite often.

This particular day Lazarus was having a very hard time getting his breath. In fact, he was in his bed when Jesus arrived.

Lazarus was sad because he did not think he could make the journey. He had really been looking forward to taking the trip.

As soon as Jesus arrived that day, he immediately walked over to Lazarus' bed. As we all watched, Jesus very gently laid his hands on Lazarus' chest.

At that very moment, Lazarus coughed a very deep cough and his breath became normal. They were able to go on their trip that very same day. Lazarus could breathe normally for months after that.

This kind of thing happened more than once. Lazarus would be well for months and then get sick again. Jesus made him well several times.

We wondered why Jesus did not just totally heal Lazarus. I could not understand why Jesus would let him continue to get sick. Somehow, we all knew that Jesus could completely heal Lazarus if he wanted to.

One day I asked Jesus about that. "Jesus is there something else Lazarus needs to do, or is there sin in our lives that is keeping you from healing him totally? I know you could do it if you wanted to."

Jesus answered, "This is not for you to know right now. One day you will certainly see Lazarus healed, and there will be many people who will witness that day with you."

Sometimes he said the weirdest things, but we all had learned that it did no good to say anything else. When he was ready, Jesus would tell us or show us, but not one minute before.

Waiting was one of the hardest things I had to learn. It caused me unnecessary grief more than once.

Looking back, I realize that Jesus had a much bigger plan for all of us. I know now, too, that we would not have believed it if Jesus had even hinted at what was to come.

CHAPTER 6

A MOST PRECIOUS GIFT

I still makes me smile to remember that beautiful day. Lazarus and I were in our late-teen years. Jesus had taken a very long trip. He was gone for over a year.

He came to see us not long after he returned. Jesus had quite a tale to tell, and two important gifts for me.

Jesus told us the same story about the magi that Papa had told all those years ago, but Jesus knew all the details. Jesus said that the wise men had visited his parents when he was about a year old.

His mother, Mary, had told the story to Jesus when he was old enough to understand and remember it. Jesus talked about the gifts these men had given, the gold, myrrh, and Frankincense.

It turned out that not only had the Magi given those gifts, but they had also left a map with Mary and Joseph. The men had told Mary that if she and Joseph should ever need help, they could use the map to find them.

Jesus had taken that map, and made the journey to find these men. That is why we had not seen him for quite some time. He had been in a faraway country.

He said he wanted these men to know how important the gifts had been. Those gifts had provided for him and his parents when they had fled to Egypt. In a very real way, the gifts saved their lives.

It was about this time that I really began to ponder about who Jesus really was. Maybe he was the promised leader that would set us free from the Romans' rule.

After all, Herod had suspected that the baby born in Bethlehem was a threat to his kingship, and might possibly jeopardize his standing with the Roman government. I was able to put this all-together much later.

Jesus was always interested in what we were doing, so that day I wanted him to see how my herb garden was flourishing.

We walked around to the side of the house where my garden was growing and where my little Olive tree and the Date Palm kept the midday sun from scorching the herbs.

That day most of the herbs were in bloom, the foliage was lush, and I was very proud of my beautiful garden. The Lavender was especially fragrant that afternoon.

Jesus said to me, "Mary, I brought two gifts from the East just for you." He opened a leather satchel and drew out a small blue bag.

"This first one is a bag of Indigo seeds. I know how you love your herbs and flowers, and you must have seen the beautiful colors made from the Indian Indigo plants. I thought you might like to try your hand at making that beautiful dye. I have carefully tended these little seeds all the way back home."

Jesus continued, "I even purchased the lovely Blue cloth bag colored with Indigo dye. It has protected the seeds on my journey. I hope you can plant them, nurture the plants, and make them multiply. Maybe you can learn to make the Indigo dye too. Now, this other gift is even more fragrant than your beautiful lavender blooms."

I did not know what to say. He had thought of me in that faraway place. What a perfect gift for me - seeds to grow lovely, useful flowers. What could be more thoughtful than that?

He reached back into the pouch, and brought forth an intricately carved alabaster jar filled with Spikenard.

"I want you to have this", he said. "One of the Magi gave it to me when I was in his country."

"I can't take this, Jesus, it is too valuable," I replied, "You could sell it. I am sure it is worth

a year's wages; even the jar must be worth a lot of money. You might need that money someday."

I just knew in my heart that he could be the one to lead a revolt against the Romans who had killed my mother and caused us all kinds of grief.

"Mary, it's important that you keep it. You will know what to do with it when the time comes."

Without another word, he placed the jar in my hands, turned, and walked back into the house. I stood there in total awe of this young man and his gifts.

I hurried to my secret place. This place was a little nook behind a loose stone in my room. I had found the loose stone one day, and hollowed out a small space there for things I wanted to keep hidden. There was a stairway to my room from outside, so no one saw me enter my room that day.

The jar fit perfectly inside the hiding place, and there is where it would stay until I would need it. The jar's seal was wax. I was sure it would be safe. After all, it survived Jesus' trip all the way across the country.

I was afraid for Martha to know that I had the Spikenard. I was certain that she would want to sell it and purchase something practical

with the money. I just knew that Jesus would need it again when he would lead the insurrection against Rome.

Little did I know that this jar would someday make me famous, and it had everything to do with God's purpose for my life!

As for the Indigo seeds, I could never have imagined how important they would become for others, as well as for myself.

CHAPTER 7

THE ESSENES

We only saw Jesus a few times, as we were approaching our early adult years. I was nearly 18 years old when Jesus came to tell us he was going to be studying with the Essenes.

We had all heard rumors about the Essenes; they were a group of devout men who lived in the hills near the desert. They took a vow of purity, and lived their lives pouring over the written Word of God. There were rumors that they might be politically connected to some of the groups that were plotting to overthrow the Roman government.

These same men had helped Jesus when he made his trip to find the wise men. Jesus said he stayed with the Essenes both on his way to the East, and on the return trip home. Jesus said that their home had been a place to rest. I wondered about that because we had heard they were political radicals. Somehow, I could not see radicals as being peaceful.

The day of Jesus' visit was sunny and bright, so we all sat in the garden where we could enjoy the breeze that was blowing through the leaves of the olive tree.

Nathan was there with us. Yes, the same Man that Martha had loved as a young girl.

Nathan was still unmarried, and he was a frequent visitor to our home.

I knew he and Martha loved each other still, and I hoped that one day she would be free to marry Nathan. She never talked about that to us. That was just Martha, never wanting to be a worry to anyone. Always concerned about others more than herself – well almost, but that again must wait until later in the story.

I remember Jesus calling our attention to a particularly beautiful bird song that he heard. It always amazed me how much he loved nature and animals. Many men would never have noticed that bird singing, or thought to share the joy of it with the rest of us. That was another reason we all loved him so much.

Jesus, like other Jewish boys, had been required to memorize the Torah. The Torah comprised the writings of Moses; it is comprised of five books.

If these boys intended to go on to be a teacher or Rabbi, they had to memorize all the books of the law in addition to these first five.

After that, an experienced rabbi would invite them to be one of his followers. These boys would learn how to teach other people to interpret the laws and writings.

There was always much discussion and trading of opinions among disciples and their Rabi.

These young men would literally walk in their rabbi's footsteps. They went where he went, ate what he ate, and tried to remember every word he spoke.

To this day, Jewish men and rabbis, in particular, love to spend their time discussing, and sometimes arguing, over the holy writings and the books of law.

Jesus was no different. He had been studying for several years by the time he was twelve. I am sure he already had memorized the Torah when I first heard him in the temple all those years ago.

Jesus had chosen to study with the Essenes, or maybe they choose him, I really do not know for sure. Maybe his rabbi might also have been a member of the Essenes.

He came to tell us that he would not have much time to visit because of all the study he would be doing.

We knew how he dearly loved discussing God's Word and telling others about it, but we all thought he was making a big mistake this time.

Martha especially tried to talk him out of going. She said that those men were radical and people would judge Jesus as being some sort of weird religious fanatic. Besides, his family probably needed his help in their Carpenter shop. Joseph had died a few years before and Jesus' and his brothers had continued the family business.

He did not even try to defend himself, he just quietly said, "It's what I have to do. My cousin John is already there and I will join him."

We had heard about his cousin but had never met him. We wondered if this was all John's idea, never the less, there was not much we could say about it. Believe me if there had been anything we could say, Martha would have tried it.

When Jesus spoke in that manner, we all knew it was useless to try to persuade him otherwise.

I secretly hoped that he might learn what to do to fight those Romans while he was there. I knew his brothers were perfectly capable of taking care of the carpentry business as well as caring for Mary, Jesus' mother.

I guess He had been gone for nearly a year before we saw him again. This time he brought his cousin, John with him.

John was even wilder than when we first met him. His hair was long and tangled; he was wearing a cloak made of goat hair spun into yarn. John reminded me of a wild animal but I kept that opinion to myself.

I thought Martha was going to have a fit! Thank goodness, she held her tongue, and served them all with grace.

I helped her as much as I could, mostly so she would not go off on a tangent, and say something she might regret later. Besides, it had been so long since we had seen Jesus that I did not want the visit marred in any way.

Jesus told us a bizarre story that his mother Mary had told about John and John's mother, Elizabeth.

It seems that Mary had gone to visit Elizabeth. Mary was in the first months of her own pregnancy.

Elizabeth was expecting John, and when Elizabeth first heard Mary's voice, her own baby jumped wildly in her womb. It was as if that baby knew who Jesus was before he was even born.

Both John and Jesus had been living, and studying with the Essenes for almost a year by this time.

We thought John was rather strange. He was tall and sinewy with wild long hair and piercing black eyes. He was very intent on his studies, and seemed driven by some unknown task that he felt was calling him.

He was a certainly a seeker, and we did not quite know what to say to him.

We finally did figure John out, but it was several years after this first visit.

We did not see Jesus again for a long time. When next we saw him, it was by a river, and it would be a life-changing event.

CHAPTER 8

A WOMAN NAMED LYDIA

While Jesus was staying with the Essenes, I was busy cultivating the Indigo plants that had grown from the seeds that Jesus had given to me. Jesus was correct about how fast they would multiply

Soon I had enough plants to fill the big plot of land that Father had taken in trade a couple of years before he died. It was not far from our home, and a perfect place to grow Indigo.

I had seen the beautiful color that the dye from these plants produced. It was rather expensive, but the Romans did not seem to mind paying the price.

I had no idea how to produce the dye, so I began to look for a way to learn the process. I could not find anyone nearby who could teach me.

Lazarus had followed Papa's example. He continued the buying and selling of fine merchandise.

Quite a bit of what Lazarus sold in that little market were items that the Romans coveted: fine leather goods, the indigo colored cloth, and other items that only the wealthy could afford.

I was about to give up on the indigo dye when a caravan from Macedonia came through our little town.

Lazarus often traded with these merchants. One of the travelers was the agent of a woman named Lydia.

She was a dealer in the blue and purple cloth and the dye that produced the lovely color.

The agent saw my fine field of Indigo, so he hired a servant to bring him back to Bethany to talk to me.

I think he had been a little surprised to find that the owner of those plants was a woman, but in view of the fact that he was delivering cloth produced by a woman, my gender did not seem to bother him much.

He said he was sure his mistress would be interested in buying dye from my plants.

When I told him I was not sure how to process the blooms, he offered to have his employer send someone to me as a teacher. He said he was sure I would be hearing from Lydia soon. Of course, I agreed. I was truly ecstatic, and could hardly wait.

Within the year, Lydia herself came from Thyatira with an entourage of servants and companions.

We were the talk of the whole area. She stayed in Jerusalem during her visit, but spent several nights in our home too.

 Lydia was a small dark-haired woman. She was dressed in indigo blue robes, her hair covered with a finely woven scarf of matching Indigo blue.

I thought she was one of the most intriguing women I had ever met, and I still do.

She taught me all I needed to know about the process of making dye from my plants, and she helped me acquire the other items I would need for making the blue color. Lazarus provided me with the funds to purchase all those things.

Since the dye was in great demand, she wanted all I could produce. I cannot tell you how excited we all were about that.

Over the years, Lydia and I have become good friends as well as business companions. We have a lot in common. My little business is successful because of the things that Lydia has taught me.

My Indigo did so well that in just a few years, I was able to pay Lazarus back the money that he had loaned to me.

Lydia was a widow. Her husband had died in battle not long after they were married.

His family was very wealthy, and Lydia was a little headstrong (like me). Lydia managed to convince the matriarch of her late husband's family to finance her indigo business.

She had been interested in flowers, herbs and plants all her life, and as she told it to me, the husband's mother was glad to have Lydia independent and no burden for the family of the dead son. In addition to all that that, they both knew how sought after the indigo dye would be.

Lydia was also very interested in our belief in one God.

She asked many questions, and we talked way into the night with Lazarus and his fellow Torah students.

She was quick to understand the concept of one God. I think if she had stayed longer, she might have converted to our way of life. However, before that could happen, the time came for her to return to Macedonia. She had many obligations there, but she promised to return as soon as she could.

She kept that promise, and over the years, I saw her many times. We kept in touch via letters that we sent back and forth with the caravans that transported the dye and supplies.

Years later, she did become a follower of Jesus, after she met the great teacher, Paul. She met Paul on one of his missionary journeys to Thyatira.

Paul said she was one of the first persons he spoke to who truly understood, and believed that Jesus was the Savior God had sent to the world.

Lydia helped financially to support Paul's trips as he traveled about telling others about Jesus.

I am sure that Jesus knew all this would happen when he brought those seeds to me.

Not only were we instrumental in helping Lydia learn God's ways, but she has been instrumental in helping me learn the trade that has provided a great source of income for my family and me. She has been a blessing for many other people also.

Because the Romans were so proud, and wanted the fine blue cloth that weavers made using our dye, we enjoyed some favor and protection. Even so, we still were always careful whenever the Romans were concerned.

My business grew, and I eventually bought a larger plot of land on the outskirts of town. I also had to add some buildings for making the actual dye.

Jesus' father, Joseph, supervised the men who did the construction for me. I was so glad about that later because Joseph got very sick and died not too long after my project was completed. I was grateful to have known him. He was so kind and full of wisdom.

People all over our region respected him. He was a good man, as well as an excellent carpenter and stonemason.

My little business helped many people in our region. I needed workers, so I hired local people to help me cultivate the plants, as well as process the dye.

One of the reasons I never married was because I was too busy to take care of a husband and children. Martha and Lazarus knew I would be all right alone, so they did not object when I was off wandering through the flowers.

That may have caused some gossip in the community, but I never cared much about what other people said.

Many people did care for me. Besides, Martha appreciated the extra income from my plants.

At the time, I thought I would be able to give support to Jesus if he were to lead a revolt against Rome. The abuse of our people was getting worse every day. It was nothing to see gruesome executions of anyone who even looked like they might disobey a Roman. Romans treated Jews with disdain, and often conscripted Jews to work on whatever projects Rome might need brute labor to complete.

The processing of the Indigo leaves involved soda ash from the Dead Sea, so we often had to visit Magdala, a seaport city where many merchants bought, sold, traded and shipped Indigo dye and its components.

It was there that I became acquainted with a woman named Mary; she was called Mary Magdalene because of her home city.

Mary would become very important to me as well as to Jesus and his friends. She and I had some wonderful times together and supported

each other through one of the worst periods of
our lives.

CHAPTER 9

ATTACKED!

Not all Romans were impressed with our Indigo. In fact, we all had to be very cautious when any Roman was around. We never knew when one of them might decide to make an example of us.

Because I was an unmarried Jewess, I had to be extra careful. I had no husband to stand up for me. Maybe that is why one of the lower ranked Roman guards thought it would be an easy thing to take advantage of me.

He would intentionally ride by my fields and watch the workers. I had advised my laborers to be as respectful as possible to any Roman who came around. This particular guard seemed to be watching and waiting for something.

One day I visited the fields to check on the plants, and see if my helpers needed anything.

I had never gone there alone, but that day all the people who would usually escort me were away or busy. I am rather impatient, a fault that has often been my downfall. That day I decided to ride out alone. I should have known better.

At any other time, there would have been someone working in the fields. It was early in the season. The plants did not need tending yet, and most of the helpers were inside working with the dye.

I had no sooner gotten off the pony and started into the field, than that same nosy Roman guard came riding down the road.

I was so busy looking at the condition of the land, that I did not see the guard come around the curve. Just as I dismounted, He galloped right up to me, grabbed my arm, and tried to pull me up onto the horse he was riding.

I panicked, and started to kick and scream. My poor little pony was frightened too, and it ran to the far side of the field. This only made the Roman more aggressive. There is no telling what would have occurred if a legion commander had not ridden around that same bend in the road, and saw what was happening. He shouted orders to the soldier to let me go or face the consequences.

The soldier dropped me right there in the middle of the dirt and galloped off as fast as his steed would run.

I was scared and bruised, but otherwise unharmed. The Captain stopped, helped me up, and gave me a strict lecture about going out alone, "Not only is it unseemly for a woman to be out alone, it is very dangerous too. If I had not shown up you may have been assaulted or even killed, and no one would have known what happened!"

He said his name was Gavius, and to use his name if I ever was in trouble with a Roman soldier again.

He then helped me catch my poor scared pony, and made sure someone came out to be with me before he left.

I could not thank him enough! I promised I would never to do that again, and I offered to send some of our Indigo dye to his home. He said that he lived in another province, and he would not be back to his home for quite some time. Besides, he said that he was not married, and he did not have time to weave. We actually had a little laugh about that. He was a very kind man.

That incident taught me that not all Romans were bad, but the ones that were could be very dangerous. Needless to say, I never went alone to my fields again.

The next time Jesus came to visit, and he heard the tale of what had happened; he did a very peculiar thing. He asked me to walk out to that field with him.

By this time, the Indigo was in full bloom. The field stretched out before us like a sea of blue and pink.

I was so proud to show Jesus the beauty that had come from his gift. Thank goodness, it was not the time to ferment the blooms. That is a stinky process. I am sure the people of Bethany are glad that the field is fairly far from the outskirts of town. When the flowers are fermenting, they smell worse than a pigpen on a hot day. Thank goodness, that process does not last very long.

Jesus and I walked all around the fields. We even walked back to the perimeter of our home property.

I thought he wanted to see how his gift had multiplied. Instead, he prayed the whole time, talking to things that I could not see, commanding angels to stand guard around all the places where we walked.

He prayed for God to protect that Roman officer. Jesus called his name, and asked for blessings to come to him.

Imagine blessing a Roman. I wondered how in the world that Jesus knew that man's name. I was sure I had not mentioned it.

Another thing that seemed extraordinary to me was that Jesus called God "Father". I was a little afraid for Jesus then.

I thought God might strike him dead, right then and there, for being so familiar with our Great God.

That sounded like blasphemy to me, but I kept my mouth shut for once, and I am so glad I did.

After that day, any Roman who came past that property rode as fast as he could to get by my fields. Their horses even got skittish, as if they saw things that humans could not. To this very day, I feel safe there.

CHAPTER 10

THE WILD MAN OF GOD

There were quite a few rumors about Jesus' cousin John. We had met him a time or two. The rumors about his birth had spread all around the country.

His father, Zechariah, was a priest of the division of Abijah and his mother, Elizabeth, was a descendant of Aaron, the first of the priests of Israel.

Zechariah and Elizabeth had never been able to have children and now, she was too old to conceive a child. This was a very troublesome thing for Jewish women. Sometimes people blamed the fact that women were barren on sin in their lives. I always thought that was unfair. I had known some very devout women who had no children.

Back then, as now, the priests cast lots to see who would go into the temple, burn the incense, and pray for the nation.

The priests had cast lots, Zechariah had won the right to go into the Holy of Holies to say the prayers, and burn the incense. No one else could go into the place of incense with the priest. He was to go in alone.

Here is the story as Zachariah told it. While he was in the Holy of Holies, while the incense was burning, he was repeating the prayers. As he prayed, an angel appeared to him.

According to the story Zachariah told, he was astounded. Of course, who would not have been? God had not spoken to anyone in Israel for over 400 years. Much less sent an angel!

The angel told Zechariah that Elizabeth was going to be able to have a child, and they were supposed to name the child John.

Well, Zechariah must have temporarily lost his mind because he questioned the angel of God. A person really should not doubt what a messenger of God tells you. Especially if he appears right in front of you when you are in the holy temple. Because Zechariah did question him, that angel got rather forceful.

According to Zechariah's story, the angel said, "I am Gabriel. I stand in the presence of God, and I have been sent to speak to you and to tell you this good news and now you will be silent and not able to speak until the day this happens, because you did not believe my words, which will come true at their appointed time."[1]

---

1   Holy Bible NIV Luke 1:19-20

Can you imagine how Zechariah felt? He had to come out and try to explain to all those people outside what had happened, and he could not speak a single word.

I think they probably thought he had lost his mind. I can just imagine the hand signals and body language he tried to do in order to make the people understand what had happened. Nothing worked. I think they must have thought he had breathed too much incense.

Well, sure enough after Zechariah returned home, Elizabeth actually did become pregnant. The baby born to her and Zechariah was Jesus' cousin John.

Another strange thing happened during that time. Jesus' mother Mary, who was in the first few months of her own pregnancy, went to visit Elizabeth who was her cousin. This was before John was born.

When Mary entered the room where Elizabeth was, the baby in Elizabeth's womb began moving around something fierce.

The Holy Spirit filled Elizabeth, and she spoke a blessing over Mary. John told us that Zachariah had written down everything Elizabeth had said that day.

She had said, "Blessed are you among women, and blessed is the child you will bare!

But why am I so favored, that the mother of my Lord should come to me? As soon as the sound of your greeting reached my ears, the baby in my womb leaped for joy. [2]

At that time, not many people had understood what she was talking about, but now, years later, we know she was talking about Jesus.

Elizabeth and Zechariah's baby was born, and when it became time to circumcise him, Elizabeth and Zechariah took him to the temple for that ceremony. It was also time to name him publicly.

Zechariah was still unable to talk so when the priest asked what the name was to be, Elizabeth said, "John." Well, the priest questioned her because John was not a family name for anyone in Elizabeth or Zechariah's families. Besides, he was probably insulted that a woman had answered for Zachariah.

At that very moment, Zechariah got his voice back. His first words were, "His name will be John!"

I guess because they are related, Jesus and his cousin, John, spent time together as boys and became close friends. After all, as it turned out, they both had a mission from God.

Later when he was a very young man, John went to the desert, and stayed with the Essenes.

---

2 Holy Bible NIV Luke 1:19-20

He would go wandering around in the wilderness wearing simple clothing, sometimes barefooted, and eating a diet of locusts and wild honey. It reminded me of stories I heard from the elders about Samson, the strong man who had never cut his hair.

John continued to live this way, and because he was descended from the priestly line of Aaron, and was some sort of wild man, many people compared him to Elijah. Some even thought he might be Elijah reincarnated. I thought that was not likely, but he defiantly was more than a little strange.

John preached all around the countryside warning people that they needed to repent of their sin, and turn back to God.

He also revived the practice of baptism that various Jews had used for purification of sin. Many people followed John.

Some even thought he might be the Messiah that we had been hoping for centuries would appear.

I wondered about this too. I so wanted to see the Romans driven out of our territory. This all turned out to be much different from what any of us imagined, especially John.

CHAPTER 11

FOLLOWING JOHN

Lazarus, Martha and I had heard all the rumors about this wild man in the desert. We were sure that the wild man was John, Jesus' cousin. The same one Jesus had brought to our house once before.

We decided to go out the next time he was anywhere nearby and see for ourselves.

It was not long before we had our chance. We heard that John, the Baptizer was going toward the Jordan River near us.

We took our old donkey, Lucifer, hitched him to our little cart, and started out early one morning. We took turns leading the donkey and riding in the cart.

It was late when we got to the river. There were many people already there, so we camped out near the river for the night. Quite a few other people were camping too. We were surprised that so many people wanted to see and hear this wild man.

Early the next morning we proceeded to the river, hoping to find a place to sit and observe what was going on.

We did not have to wait long. Soon John, Jesus' cousin, came to the river with a large group of his disciples. Not much about his appearance had changed. He still wore that rough cloak and his hair was long and tangled.

What had changed was his demeanor. Before, he had been soft-spoken, and a little shy. Now he was bold, almost fierce, and spoke with conviction.

He talked about how we needed to repent of our sin, give up our love of material things, and our lack of compassion for others.

He talked about how we had made a mockery of God's law. He said we had added laws for ourselves. Laws to make us look better than we actually are. He said we did not seem to care what God's word said about all that either.

John said we should repent, and be baptized because the Messiah was coming soon. Jews have been looking for the Messiah for centuries, and most of us had nearly given up.

I have to say, John inspired us. I could see why some people thought he might be Elijah, the prophet from long ago.

Lazarus especially listened intensely to what John was calling for us to do.

All at once, our brother took off toward the river as if he were on a mission. He got in line with the others who were waiting in the shallow water for John to baptize them.

Mary and I watched as Lazarus prayed, and asked God to forgive him for not being the man he should have been. John dunked Lazarus right under the water and our brother came up laughing for joy!

I could not believe my eyes when Martha started running toward the river too. She also stood in line. Then John baptized her too. That left me alone on that little rise of ground near the water.

I began to remember all the times I had been less than kind to Martha and the hate I had for that Roman soldier who ran over mama. I remembered my jealousy because Lazarus had more freedom than I did, just because he was a man.

It was then that I realized I needed to ask for forgiveness too. I was afraid, and more than a little embarrassed to follow my brother and sister into the water. However, a strange force seemed to be compelling me forward.

I got at the end of the line and waited for my turn. I grew more nervous the longer I stood there.

Of course, the longer I stood there the more I feared how foolish I would look if I ran back to my place on the hill.

Running back was just what I wanted to do! The fear of looking foolish was greater than the fear of John, so I stayed in line with the others.

Soon it was my turn. I slowly walked into the water. John met me, held my hands in the kindest way and said, "My little sister, Mary, do you want to turn from your sin, ask God to forgive you, and help you to be the woman He wants you to be?"

At that moment, I knew I wanted that more than anything else I could think of.

"Yes," I whispered, and John lowered me under the water.

When I came up, I felt like all my sin had flowed down with the river current. I wanted to dance out of that water! I would have too, but I figured Martha would make me walk all the way home for embarrassing her.

It was a hot sunny day, so being wet was not so bad. We stayed to hear more of what The Baptizer had to say and we were soon dry.

It was getting toward afternoon. We were thinking it was time to start back, when we were shocked to see Jesus standing on the riverbank.

Jesus started into the river toward John, but John said to him, "What are you doing? You should be baptizing me."

We all wondered about that, but Jesus said, "No, I need to do this now to fulfill everything that is right." We were even more perplexed, but John reluctantly agreed.

He baptized Jesus, and then a very strange thing happened. Jesus and John stood and looked up into the sky as if they were seeing something -

Something that no one else could see or hear. The way the light was shining on them it appeared as if they were glowing.

I heard what sounded like thunder, but there were no clouds. Then we saw a bird, a dove, come out of nowhere and light on Jesus' shoulder. Neither Jesus nor John seemed the least bit surprised by that.

Soon everything was normal again. The bird flew away, and Jesus was walking toward us.

I wondered if I had imagined that whole thing, but Lazarus and Martha told me later that they had seen it too. There was something different about Jesus. There was an aura of peace and a feeling of power surrounding him.

He stopped briefly to speak to us. He told Lazarus that he had somewhere he needed to go, and it would be a while before we would see him again.

Jesus was so happy when he found out that John had baptized us; he hugged us all, and then walked away. We did not see him again for quite some time.

Jesus never did talk to us about where he went after that day.

We would not know for several years what had happened to him during that time. He did not talk to us about where he had been, nor how important the decisions he made while he was there would be for everyone.

CHAPTER 12

CHANGES

I think after that day on the river we all felt like new people. I for sure had a peace and calm that I had not experienced before. I began to think a lot about what I might do to make a difference with my life. What could I do to help other people? Was there something special God wanted me to do?

The only answer seemed to keep doing what I normally did every day, and look for opportunities to help, encourage, or love someone else. All that would end up being quite a challenge.

The Roman soldier who had tried to harm me showed up again. This time he was not in my field. He was guarding a caravan. The caravan would carry our dye to Lydia. Zilla and I were in Jerusalem, and the guard saw us coming. I was standing there beside one of my helpers. We were overseeing the loading of the vats of dye onto the carts.

I saw the solider watching, and my heart began to beat a little faster. It was not all fear this time; it was also a feeling of compassion. I wondered how I could be feeling sympathy for the man who had jerked me off my pony, and would have hurt me for sure.

The feeling would not go away, but I knew I needed to use caution and common sense as well.

When the men with me had finished loading all the dye onto the carts, and before we all left, I turned to the guard and simply said, "Thank you for making sure my dye is being kept safe. It means a lot for me to know that I don't need to worry about it getting lost or stolen."

My heart was pounding so hard I thought for sure he could hear it. The look on his face said it all. It was as if no one had ever thanked him before. He did not speak, only nodded, but I still knew in my heart that I had done the right thing. It made me feel good to have spoken to him. Was it really so simple?

I also noticed a difference at home. Oh, I still would rather read or listen to the men debate the Torah than to cook or clean, but I did tell Mary how much I enjoyed her wonderful cooking. I tried not to grumble as much when she really needed my help. She did not seem to be quite the perfectionist that she once was either. I could see she was changing just as I was.

Lazarus also changed. He got very serious about studying of the Torah after our time at the river. He began to debate with the other men about the meaning of the ancient laws.

I loved to hear them expound on what they thought about these laws. It was interesting to hear them argue over how we needed to apply those laws in our everyday lives.

At least two new moons had passed since our baptism in the river. We looked up one day, and Jesus was walking up the hill to our house. He was with four men who I had never seen before.

Of course, Martha always had some sort of treat in the kitchen, so Lazarus invited them in for a cool drink and some refreshment.

Jesus introduced us to Simon Peter, Peter's brother Andrew and to Phillip and Nathaniel. Jesus said they were fishermen from Galilee, and they were his disciples.

It was obvious that they were hanging on every word that Jesus spoke. Our dear friend Jesus had become a Rabbi – a teacher of the Torah. I was so happy about that and proud that he wanted us to meet his followers. They all would always be welcome in our home.

There was also something different about Jesus. He was not the same person whom John had baptized in the Jordan River.

I know he was a respected rabbi, but it was more than that. I could not put my finger on it, but something was definitely not the same. There was an air of authority on him, and he seemed to be much more intense than before.

We had heard that he had spent a long time in the desert. He had gone there too fast and pray.

Much later, we also learned that Satan had tempted him while he was there.

I mean literally. The evil ruler of the underworld, Satan, had tried to get Jesus to jump off the temple wall! Jesus would have been dashed to pieces if he had done that! Satan had said to Jesus, "For it is Written: 'He will command His angles concerning you, and they will lift you up in their hands, so that you will not strike your foot against a stone.[3]

Many years later, I was to understand all this much clearer, but back then, I could not possibly know what God had planned for Jesus.

Jesus had begun to tell some wonderful stories. Like many other rabbis, he made up parables to help make the laws easier to understand. He gave us advice that could have come right out of God's own mouth.

Most everyone was astounded that a carpenter's son from Nazareth could be so wise.

I knew then that he was going to become a great and famous Rabbi. What I never suspected was how Jesus, the rabbi, would literally change the lives of us all.

---

3 Psalm 91:11,12 The Narrated Bible

CHAPTER 13

JESUS AND THE FISHERMEN

One day when Jesus was teaching near the Sea of Galilee. So many people were trying to be near him that it had become hard for him to walk, much less teach.

Jesus was standing near two fishing boats. The boats just happened to belong Simon Peter and his brother Andrew. The men who had visited with Jesus in our home.

They were cleaning and drying their nets. He asked Peter, if he could use his boat as a place from which to teach. Simon agreed, and he pushed the boat out a little into the lake, so that everyone could see and hear.

Because of the hills that surround the shore of the Sea of Galilee, a boat was a perfect place to teach. The place was almost like being in the Roman coliseum. Everyone could hear Jesus speaking.

After Jesus finished teaching, he said to Simon, "Let's go fishing." Simon said, "We have fished all night. We didn't catch a single fish, but if you really want to, I will put our nets out again"

When I heard this story, I could just imagine what Peter was thinking.

Here it was morning; he and his fellow fishermen had fished all night and no fish.

These men earned their living fishing. They knew when it was time to hang up their nets.

Nevertheless, they pushed out into the deeper water, and Simon dropped the net down. As soon as it had sunk, the net was full! There were so many fish that he could not pull it into the boat. He called for his brother, Andrew, who was in another boat to come help. The fish were so plentiful that both boats were so full that they nearly sank from the weight.

This was so astounding, that Simon and his companions fell to their knees in fear. They knew they were in the presence of someone extraordinary.

Jesus said to them, "Leave your nets and follow me and I will make you fishers of men."[4]

Without a second glance back, Simon left his boat and nets with his helpers, and he set out with Jesus.

A little farther down the shore were two more fishermen who also had witnessed this miracle.

Jesus said to these men, "Come go with us." They also dropped their nets, and went along with Simon, his men, and Jesus.

All these men, Simon Peter (we just called him Peter), his brother Andrew, and their friends James and John became good friends of our

---

4 Matthew 4:19 NASB

family. James and John were brothers as well. It was getting to be a family thing.

None of these men ever got tired of telling the story of that huge catch of fish.

Peter especially loved talking and telling stories. He did not have a shy bone in his body. He would stop and talk to anyone who would listen. In the years to come, this turned out to be a wonderful gift for Peter.

They all went together to Capernaum, and Peter took Jesus to his home to meet his family.

Peter went ahead to let his mother-in-law know that there would be guests. When he arrived, he found that she was sick in bed with a bad fever.

When Jesus and the others arrived, the women told Jesus that she was sick, probably to warn him that she could not prepare a meal, or perhaps they thought he could heal her. Everyone had heard the stories about the people Jesus had healed.

Jesus went into the room where Peter's mother was in bed.

He took her by the hand. Peter said that at that very moment she was well, just like that. Sick one moment, up and bustling around preparing a meal the next.

Word about her healing got around town very quickly and before the night was over everyone in town, who was sick, were coming to Peter's house for healing. There were even people who had been demon possessed that were set free from those demons.

CHAPTER 14

A WEDDING WE WILL NEVER FORGET

I guess I need to explain a little about Jews in general. Jews were wanderers for a long time before God gave us a place to live. Our ancestors had wandered around in the desert for forty years after their escape from Egypt. They were waiting for God to lead them into the Promised Land. Of course, their own sin had been the reason for that forty-year journey.

Anyway, maybe because of that long-ago trip in our history; we do not have any problem traveling fairly far to see friends and relatives. We are scattered all over Judea, so a day's walk is no big deal for us, especially if a celebration would be involved.

I love parties. The best parties are when someone gets married. The feast and merry making go on for over a week.

Not long after our baptism, there was a wedding in Cana, and we were all invited.

This was soon after we had met the first four of Jesus' new followers, the four fishermen; Peter, Andrew, Phillip and Nathanael. We invited them to come with us.

Martha planned and supervised wonderful parties and feasts. Many people all over the region asked her to oversee their celebrations.

This time it was our cousin who was getting married.

His family was one of the families we had traveled with long ago to Jerusalem for the infamous Passover.

The Passover when Jesus helped me after I got into trouble in the temple.

Martha was in charge of the celebration. She and a few friends had gone ahead of us to prepare for the wedding feast.

There would be much food, wine and lots of fun. About four days into this celebration, Mary, Jesus' mother, noticed that the wine was almost gone.

I do not know why she went to Jesus instead of Martha, but it turned out to be the best thing she could have done. She told Jesus that the wine was running out. More people had come than anyone had expected.

Martha was horrified! She just knew her reputation was ruined. I do not know why she did not realize that the problem was not her fault. The problem was the uninvited guests who had come to the feast.

Martha's friend Nathan was one of the invited guests, and I wondered if Martha was embarrassed because Nathan might think this was her mistake.

It was then that Jesus said something very strange to his mother. He said, "Woman, what do you expect me to do? My time has not yet come.[5]"

I totally understood the "what do you expect me to do" part. Did she want him to go buy more wine, or try to explain to everyone what had happened? It was the "My time has not yet come" that made no sense at all.

I will never forget what Jesus did next. He turned to one of the servants and said, "See those water vessels over there? Go fill them up with water from the well."

The water jars were the great big ones used for ceremonial washing before a sacrifice or a sacred fast. I thought he was going to try to serve water instead of wine. I did not think that was going to work at all. The guests had not drunk so much wine that they would not notice that!

It took three servants to carry all the jars and fill them with water.

When they got back with them, Jesus said, "Now draw out some of it, and take a cup of it to the wedding master for him to taste."

That was the weirdest thing. I just knew the Wedding Master is going to think he had lost his

---

5 Holy Bible John 2:4

mind for giving him water to taste. Martha could not even bear to look!

When the wedding Master had tasted the water (or what we thought was water), he exclaimed, "This is the best wine I've ever tasted! Most people serve the good wine first, and when everyone is getting a little tipsy, they bring out the cheap wine, but you have saved the best wine till last!"

Jesus had somehow turned that water into wine! Something was going on that we did not understand. Martha was so relieved because Jesus had saved her reputation.

I pondered about all of this for quite some time. I also wondered what he meant when he told his mother that it was not his time yet. What time? Was there something she knew that we did not? Was he going to help her with the parties now? How could he do that, and continue to be a rabbi and teach all these men about God's Law?

I began to realize that there was much more about Jesus than we had ever imagined. It was not until he had many people following him all over the countryside, that I begin to see there was something completely different about this Rabbi.

CHAPTER 15

A TRIP WITH JESUS

Jesus had chosen several young men to come and travel with him, and there were lots more following him around who just showed up wherever he went.

All Rabbis had groups of men and some women, who followed them from place to place, and listened to what they taught.

Rabbis gathered in groups, discussed the Torah, and enjoyed arguing with each other about different ways to interpret the written laws and the words of the prophets. I, also, sat and listened as often as I could.

I could not actually call myself Jesus' disciple, because I was not free to follow him wherever he went. I sat at his feet every time I got a chance to listen. I loved to join in those discussions too. I had heard many teachers, but He was the best. I guess many other people must have thought so too, because numerous people started gathering when he would stop to teach.

After the wedding in Cana, we all went to Capernaum for a few days. Jesus and his disciples went with us. We wanted Martha to rest after the wedding party. While we walked, we began to talk about many of the things that were going on in the temple.

We discussed how some people did not have to nurture a lamb from birth, spend the day shopping for one at market, or purchase a dove to take to the temple on sacrifice day. People could just go to a booth in the outer court of the temple, purchase anything they might need, and the priest would perform the sacrifice.

We wondered what God might be thinking of merchants buying and selling in the temple courts. We felt like it might disrespectful of God's house.

When we raised a little lamb from its birth, or had to search for a perfect lamb in the market place, the sacrifice became much more personal.

I remember that father had us keep the lamb that we had raised near us, and it really became like a pet. It broke our hearts when we had to watch it die to pay for our sins each year. That made us see how our sin hurt God too. I had always wished that there could have been another way to get forgiveness for our sins.

I could see that Jesus was beginning to get a little annoyed about all the buying and selling.

He said it was the house of God, and the merchants were disrespecting God and the law to turn God's house into a market place.

It was not as if they could not buy sacrificial animals in the market place right outside the Holy Temple. It was full of vendors who sold all sorts of things, including animals, which were required for the sacrifice.

After all that conversation was finished, we started for home. We arrived back at our home. Jesus and his followers left us there and headed out for Jerusalem.

Later we learned that Jesus went straight to the temple. He was very angry. He turned over the merchant's tables, scattering money and animals all over the place. The priests' and the guards were astounded! He shouted at them, "You have made my Father's house into a den of thieves!"

We all thought of God as our heavenly Father, but I sensed that Jesus understood Him as something quite different.

No ordinary Rabbi would ever have been so bold, and especially would not have dared to call God "Father."

Some Jews were thinking Jesus might be the Messiah. God had promised us a savior who would deliver us from all our enemies.

I guess the chief priests and the temple guards did not think Jesus was this man, because they were very upset that he had wrecked the market place in the outer court.

Everyone knew that most of the priests and temple rulers liked the market there because the vendors paid a big fee for the privilege to sell there. Most of that payment lined the pockets of the Pharisees and Sadducees.

It is amazing that they did not arrest Jesus. Friends told us that he just seemed to disappear into the crowd after he turned over all the tables and scattered animals everywhere! The guards looked rather foolish trying to figure out what had happened.

I secretly was very happy about all that. Those men had intimidated me once or twice also. I sure was beginning to hope that our deliverer had finally come. The Jewish rulers were not a happy crowd. Looking back, I think this is where all the trouble began.

CHAPTER 16

A DISCIPLE PROBLEM A HAPPY ENDING

While Jesus and his followers had been teaching and traveling around the countryside, his cousin John was teaching also. They both had many followers. Some of John's words were quite bold.

I actually saw him get right in the face of a tax collector. Tax collectors were a bunch of scoundrels, everyone knew it, but no one was brave enough to say it to their faces except John.

These men collected taxes, and always overcharged and kept the extra money for themselves. The authorities knew what they were doing, but let them get away with it. Probably because they got a cut of the money as well.

John told the tax collectors right to their faces that they should only collect what was due. They should give to the Romans only what the taxes actually were and not collect one penny more. The tax collectors did not like that one bit. I think they must have complained to the temple authorities too.

Jesus was teaching a little different. He taught about loving our neighbor.

He taught that we needed to treat others the same way we would want them to treat us.

He said we should share what we have with other people, especially the ones who were less fortunate than we were.

That one hit home to me. My indigo fields had provided a fine wage for me, and I realized I needed to share some of my money and products with other women. I was sure there were women who needed cloth for a robe or money for food. I started to watch for ways to share my blessings.

One day Jesus was teaching on a hillside. He was teaching about our blessings and about how to love others.

Martha, Lazarus and I were there that particular day. We loved to hear Jesus talk and explain the sacred writings for us, so we went to hear him as often as we could.

Not everyone was pleased about Jesus. A few of John's disciples were disturbed because Jesus' followers were baptizing people as a symbol of repenting of their sins in the same way John did.

The story was that some of John's disciples went to John and told him that a lot people were beginning to follow Jesus. More than were following John.

I really had to ponder on what John had said to them.

He told the ones who were concerned that Jesus was going to take his followers away, "I told you that I am not the Christ! Remember that I said I was the one to announce the one who is greater than I am? The bride belongs to the bridegroom and the friend who waits and listens for him to arrive is full of joy at his appearance! I am that one who waits. That joy is mine and is now complete. The one we have waited for is here! "[6]

Some of John's disciples must have understood what John had said that day because, after that, some of John's disciples started following Jesus.

About that same time, some of the Pharisees noticed that Jesus was getting more followers than John. No one really wanted those people to take notice of anything, especially a growing popularity.

Pharisees were a jealous bunch who wanted to control as much as they could. Jesus must have thought it would be better for him and his people to go somewhere else for a while.

He decided to go back to Galilee. The quickest way back was through Samaria. The disciples did not want to go that way, because Jews did not associate with Samaritans.

It was a race thing. Most Jews thought Samaritans were not as good as they were. I have to admit, I believed it too. I was about to change my mind about that in a big way.

Never the less, Jesus insisted that they were going to go through Samaria.

Peter said this is what happened that day:

When they were almost there, the disciples stopped to buy food. Jesus went ahead of them into the town of Sychar.

It was nearly noon and very hot. Jesus knew there was a well outside the city. Our ancestor, Jacob, had dug the well. Jacob later gave it to his son, Joseph. Jesus stopped at this well to get a drink.

It was the very hottest time of day, and normally no one would have been out in the heat. There was a woman drawing up water. Jesus did not have a way to draw up the water, so he asked if she would draw him a drink.

She was surprised, and asked him why a Jew would drink water that a Samaritan had drawn. In fact, she was surprised that a Jew was even in Samaria.

According to the disciples, Jesus had a long discussion with her. He told her many things about herself that no stranger could have possibly known.

He told her that she was not married. He also said that she was living with a man who was not her husband.

Jesus said to her that he had living water, so that she would never be thirsty again. He also told her that a time was coming when everyone would worship God in spirit and truth – even Jews and Samaritans together!

She said to him that she knew about the coming Messiah, and that the Messiah would teach everyone what is true. Jesus actually said to her, "I am that Messiah."

It was about that time that the disciples returned with food, and the woman had run off to tell everyone that she had seen the Messiah. She told the people in the town. She also said that he had told her things that he could not have possibly known about her life!

The disciples were astounded! So was half the town. That day many of the people in that town came to see for themselves, and they too believed that Jesus was truly the Messiah.

When I heard this. I was thrilled! It is what I had suspected all along!

Jesus and his disciples stayed there for two days because so many Samaritans wanted to talk to him. Many of them believed his story.

I am not too sure that Jesus' disciples were very pleased about that time in Samaria, but they never said so. After a few days, they made their way back to Galilee.

Jesus had realized that the woman in Samaria needed a new start, so he told her about me and my Indigo plants. He promised her that he would talk to me, and see if I would allow her to come help me in return for a place to stay. That turned out to be a wonderful relationship for her and myself as well.

CHAPTER 17

THE WOMAN AT THE WELL AND ME

It was harvest time. I was so busy that even Martha was worried about me. I needed someone to make lists and help me organize my time. I could not supervise the harvest, keep the records, and make sure all the dyeing process was working. I needed help.

Jesus had told me about Zilla, the Samaritan woman, but I had not had time to think about how to find her.

One day I had started out to check on the workers in my largest field. I had actually paused to admire the lovely view of the Indigo flowers. They were in full bloom. A great carpet of blue and pink flowers spread over the land. So beautiful! The rows hugged the curve in the road, and seemed like waves of blossoms flowing over the land. The hard work somehow seems worth it when I see the lovely flowers. I can never look at these flowers without feeling grateful to Jesus all over again.

As I was admiring the beauty of the landscape and watching the harvesters, I saw a woman riding a donkey toward me. This was rather strange because women were seldom out alone.

This woman was wearing a robe over her tunic, and she had a pack on the back of the donkey. As she rode closer, I saw that she was very pretty. Her hair was black; long and glossy, a few curls peeked out from under her head covering. She was small; in fact, she was not much bigger than a child would be.

I wondered where she might have come from or if she might be lost. She came straight up our path instead of staying on the road to Jerusalem. This woman rode right up to my helper and me. She halted her donkey, and asked, "Do you know where I might find Mary, the Indigo grower?"

I was quite surprised. "I am that Mary."

"Do you know a teacher named Jesus?" She inquired.

"He is a dear friend of my family," I said. I was quite intrigued by her questions and wondering what all this had to do with me.

"My name is Zilla. Jesus changed my life! He set me free from my sins. I was not a very good person when I happened to meet him at a well where I was drawing water.

It is a long story, and if you could just take a moment, I will tell it to you. I will make it as brief as I can. I can see how busy you are, but this Jesus said if I would find you, we may be able to help each other."

Well, you can imagine how intrigued I was. I was in a hurry, but there was something about this woman, and how her face lit up when she mentioned Jesus. I knew then, that she was probably the woman from Samaria that Jesus had said he would send.

"Come with me. I need to check on my workers, and then we can go to my house. I will make us something to drink and eat. You must be tired and hungry after your journey. You can tell me your story there."

It crossed my mind that our neighbors may not be happy because I was entertaining a Samaritan, and a woman on top of that, but I never worried too much about what people thought of me.

Zilla seemed so grateful. I found myself drawn to her in spite of her unorthodox way of showing up on a donkey in the middle of the road.

One of the workers escorted us back home after we had seen that the harvest was going as planned. Zilla was amazed at everything about the Indigo process, and she too, fell in love with the Indigo flowers.

We settled into my room with bread, cheese, fruit and tea. She began to tell me about her encounter with Jesus at Joseph's well, and all that transpired in her village because of Jesus.

Honestly, by this time I was not surprised that he had done all those things in her village.

When she told me what Jesus had said about being the Messiah, I was a little shocked. Of course, I had suspected it myself, but wondered why he had not admitted it to us, his good friends, before telling some stranger and Samaritan at that. I tried not to let my feelings show, and Zilla continued with her story.

Zilla said Jesus had mentioned my indigo dye. He had said that maybe she could be of help to me. She said that she was not afraid of hard work, and was very clever at making do without the things many people considered necessities.

She also said that she had saved a little money. She hoped it might help pay for a place to stay. Now if there was only a means of providing for her future.

"Could you use my help with your business?" She asked. "I would do anything you need. I am a quick learner. I can read and write, and I am very good with figures too. I have not always been a woman of the night. My family all died from a sickness that swept through our village when I was a young girl. I was too young to have married and the only one left of my family. I had to fend for myself. Before the sickness happened to my family, our father saw to it that all his children could read and do sums. "

Little did she know how badly I needed her help. I was thrilled that she knew how to work with numbers too. What a blessing!

I knew someone I could trust to provide a room for her until she could do better. The fact that Jesus had sent her was the seal on the deal.

"I need someone to help me with keeping records. Jesus must have known we would be good for each other. You can rest here for the day. I will speak to my friend about finding you a place to stay for a while until you can get established."

The joy on her face turned my dreary day into sunshine. That was the beginning of a lifelong relationship. I knew that no one needed to know about her past. After all, she was no longer that woman. Many people need a new start, and I was grateful that I could be the one to help her.

Zilla became indispensable to me. Our old Donkey, Lucifer, even accepted Zilla's little donkey, Eli, as his companion and stall mate.

We found Zilla a temporary room at the home of our cousins, and we began to make plans to build a little house for her on a plot of land behind our house.

There was a pretty hill there, and Jesus' brothers James, Joses, Jude, and Simon all got together and built a sweet little house for Zilla.

This time I was the one who loaned the funds for the building. Zilla was faithful to pay me back too.

She loved that home so much. Zilla enjoyed flowers and herbs as much as I. Together we planted Rosemary, Lavender and Thyme around the house. Lazarus helped us transplant a small Olive tree for her yard.

Our friend, Aaron, who was a stonemason, constructed a wonderful stone and clay oven near her back door. Zilla baked the most wonderful bread loaves in that oven. She seasoned them with her herbs. No one ever turned down an offer of Zilla's bread. Zilla and her bread changed the way many in our town felt about Samaritans.

Not only was she the perfect helper for me, but she was like a sister as well. Together we went through many life issues, both joyful and terribly painful. There were many times when I was ever so grateful that Jesus had sent her to me.

CHAPTER 18

ROMANS, ROYALTY AND MIRACLES

During all the time of building and helping to get Zilla established, something else strange was happening.

It had to do with that Roman guard to whom I had tried to be kind. He kept showing up in some of the same places where I was; in the market place, near the meeting places of my customers, sometimes I would see him on the road as my helpers and I were working. It was a little scary because Romans were always looking for excuses to inconvenience Jews.

The weirdest thing was that I was not very afraid. Maybe I should have been. If I had known then what would happen later, I might have tried to intervene.

Jesus did another amazing thing after they all got back from Samaria. He and his disciples had gone to Cana in Galilee. There must be something special about Cana.

As soon as they got back, a royal officer was waiting for them. He said to Jesus," My son is sick and dying. Please come with me because I know you can heal him."

We do not know if it was because it was a day's journey, or something else, but for some reason, this disturbed Jesus.

He said to the officer, "Unless you people see a miracle, you will never believe!"

The man was not going to give up and said, "Please just come. He may be dead by now."

Jesus said, "Go home. Your son will live."

The man believed Jesus, and started home. He had not gone more than half way before one of his servants met him and said, "The fever is gone! The boy will live!" The officer asked, "When exactly did the fever leave?"

"About this same time yesterday." The servant said. The officer realized that it had happened at the exact same time Jesus had told him his son would live.

This was the first of many people whom Jesus healed. There were so many that folks began to follow Jesus just to see the miracles, as well as find healing for themselves.

While Jesus was still in Galilee teaching and his disciples were baptizing people, news came that Herod had arrested his cousin John.

Evidently, John had accused Herod, the Tetrarch, of living with his own brother's wife. John had told a bunch of other sinful things that Herod had done too. So Herod made up some charges, had John arrested, and thrown into prison.

Some said that John had fascinated Herod. Herod often visited John in prison, and asked him many spiritual questions.

We all hoped that Herod would decide to set John free. I believe Herod would have eventually freed John if it had not been for his evil wife, Herodias.

When Jesus heard the news about John, he was very sad, but he continued to heal, and teach the people who gathered around him everywhere he went. It seemed that he never had time for himself, not even to go check on his cousin and friend.

Jesus left Galilee, and made his way to Capernaum. We did not see him for a while, but we heard word of his teaching and miracles that seemed to be happening in all the places that he went.

While he was in Capernaum, something happened that could have been the end of Jesus' mission. The story about the incident got around very quickly. Everyone wondered about what had taken place, and how Jesus managed to get away. It happened like this:

One Sabbath morning he went to the synagogue in his hometown of Nazareth. This was the very synagogue where Jesus had studied as a boy growing up.

This time while he was there, the men asked Jesus to read the Holy Scriptures. He turned to a passage in Isaiah that was predicting what would happen when the Messiah would arrive.

Jesus finished reading that passage, rolled up the scroll and sat down to teach. What he said next astounded everyone.

He said, "Today these words from the prophet have been fulfilled and you are seeing it for yourselves".[7]

The people were impressed and amazed that he said all this, but very soon someone said, "Wait a minute. Is this not Joseph the carpenter's son? We have known him all his life. He can't be so special"

What happened then was amazing! Phillip told me that Jesus said to that man, "You know, hometowns always reject their prophets. Do you remember when there was a terrible famine in the Prophet Elijah's hometown? God did not send him to help anyone from that town, but God sent Elijah to an outsider, a widow in Zarephath in Sidon. God also sent him to heal a leper who was an outsider from another city."

They knew that Jesus was the promised Messiah and they choose to reject him.

What he said really made them mad. They crowded around Jesus. They began to push him

---

7 Luke 4:21

out of the synagogue and all the way to the edge of a cliff!

They would have pushed him over the cliff, but the disciples who were there said that Jesus just seemed to disappear. He walked right through the crowd, and no one seemed to see him at all! Jesus and his friends did not return to Nazareth, but traveled to Galilee.

I was very busy with the fields and harvest during that time, and I always hoped for news from Jesus and his followers. Lazarus, Martha and I had become to love them as if they were our family. They often spent time in our home when they were in our region.

Sometimes we were lucky enough to be able to go where Jesus was teaching. It was amazing to see the crowds and hear Jesus expound on God's Holy Word.

We had been there when He healed sick and lame people. This did not surprise us at all because we had seen him heal our own brother many times.

No one else had ever done miracles like those that Jesus performed. We knew by now that he truly was the promised Messiah.

CHAPTER 19

JESUS THE TROUBLE MAKER

Zilla and I were quite busy with the harvest, and preparing the Indigo for the dye making process, so we were not always free to go where Jesus was teaching.

Jesus was getting into controversial situations nearly everywhere he went. We heard the news about him from neighbors, customers, and even first hand from Jesus and his close followers.

When they were going to and from Jerusalem they often stayed with our family, and believe me, it was always a lively and inspiring time when Jesus reclined at our table.

One afternoon, they all arrived without any warning, and Martha was in a tizzy. We had plenty of food in the garden. There was fresh goat cheese. Zilla always had a few loves of fresh bread to share and we had plenty of wine, so I did understand Martha's problem. Jesus and the men were always grateful for whatever we had to offer.

I was tired from a long day of work, and to be honest, I wanted to sit and listen to the stories of Jesus' latest adventures.

I wanted to learn what was happening as they traveled about. I was a little worried about some rumors I had been hearing. People were saying that the Temple rulers were angry because of some of the things that Jesus had said and done.

I was there, sitting on a cushion at Jesus' feet. Zilla was helping Martha, but that was not enough for Martha. She came to the door of the kitchen, hands on hips, and said to Jesus, "Do you not care at all that I am in here working to prepare a meal for all of you and Mary is sitting there without a care in the world?'

Well, I nearly fell over at his answer. I truly expected to get a reprimand, and a suggestion for me to get up and help Martha, but instead he said, "Martha, Martha, you are so worried about things that do not matter all that much. We do not mind what we eat or even if we do. Mary has chosen the best thing. She choose to sit, and spend time with me. Our time is short, and there will come a time when you will look back on this day, and wish you had chosen differently".

I did not quite understand what he meant by that last part, but I was so glad he had defended me.

We did finally eat, and then, all of us joined Jesus to hear the latest stories of their travels.

Later that evening, I helped Martha clean up, and she seemed in a better mood.

I noticed Martha spent more time listening, and she joined the conversation often in the days that followed.

Jesus and his followers stayed with us for a few days. They told us many stories of their adventures.

Peter told us that Jesus had asked a tax collector named Levi to come travel with them.

Levi accepted that invitation, and many of the people, especially temple authorities., were offended. The other disciples were a little surprised, but Peter said Levi was a good man, and seemed to be truly sorry for how he had treated his fellow Jews.

All this happened after Levi had a talk with Jesus late one night after everyone else was asleep. Levi even said he was sorry for taking more money than he should have, and he gave a lot of it to poor and sick people whom they met as they traveled.

Not only did Jesus have a tax collector as a follower, but also a little later, Levi threw a big party for Jesus. He invited all his tax collector friends and some of their companions. These people were never the most popular folks in town.

Of course, I thought that was all right. I never did like all those pretentious Jews who thought they were better than the rest of us.

Zilla loved that story as well. She could truly relate.

Never the less, I could see where this might prove to be a bad decision for Jesus. Most of us tried to keep a low profile when it came to the Pharisees and Sadducees.

Those men were all trying to keep in good standing with the Romans and temple leaders. Everyone in these groups could cause trouble for any person they decided to use as an example.

Jesus' disciples also told us a story about a man that Jesus healed on a Sabbath. We had all seen this man at the pool of Bethesda. He was very crippled, and had been there for years. I think his family may have brought him there every day in hopes that his healing would happen.

Everyone believed that sometimes an Angel would come and stir the water in the pool. The first ones into the pool after that happened received healing. I do not know if that was true or not, but there were always sick and lame people at the pool. I never saw the water move, but I know many people gave money to those sick people.

Anyway, Jesus felt sorry for this man when he saw him, and heard that he had been coming there for years.

Jesus asked the crippled man if he really wanted healing. I thought that rather strange, of course if he was there, he wanted healing.

Then it occurred to me that maybe some of those people were making more money being cripple than if they were well and had to work like the rest of us.

The man said, yes, he wanted to be healed, but he could never get into the pool in time. He said someone else always got in before he could.

Well, Jesus said to him, "Get up! Take your mat and go home."

I bet that man was surprised. He probably expected Jesus to give him money, and leave like everyone else.

The disciples said he paused a moment, felt his legs, jumped up and ran around like a crazy person!

He picked up his pallet, and started to walk away when a Pharisee stopped him. The Pharisee accused him of doing work on the Sabbath. They believed that even carrying your pallet was work.

That man told them that the one who healed him had told him to pick up his pallet. The man said he thought if Jesus could heal him, he must be a great man of God, and it would be all right to do what he said.

The Pharisee asked that man to point out the healer to him, but Jesus had slipped away, and that man did not know what Jesus' name was, or where He had gone.

Too bad Jesus could not have left that alone. He came back later, and told the man that he needed to quit sinning, or something worse might happen to him. I wondered what sin Jesus knew about.

Well, that man went straight to the Jews who had questioned him, and he told them Jesus' name. It seemed like Jesus was trying to make trouble for himself, and quite a few people were helping make that happen.

I began to worry a little about what might transpire if he kept this up. I was not sure this was the best way to lead a rebellion. He might need the help of the Jewish leaders. I was sure they wanted their freedom also. I was terribly wrong about that!

CHAPTER 20

A VISIT WE WILL NEVER FORGET

Finally, the harvest was finished, and it was time to ship our dye to the merchants.

Zilla and I were getting ready to go to the city of Magdala on the Sea of Galilee. We did not make this trip often.

I usually sent the products by caravan because it was a three-day journey and we would have needed an escort. Caravans could be dangerous because highway bandits often robbed them.

I had noticed a rather remarkable thing. Ever since Jesus had prayed over my fields and the plants, I had never lost a single drop of dye to robbers. The power of that prayer must have extended to the caravans, because we never had any trouble on our way.

We undertook this particular trip because we wanted to see our merchant friend, Mary.

On our first trip to Magdala, when we went there to sell our dye, and arrange for the transport, Zilla and I had met a very special woman.

The city of Magdala is the center of the indigo cloth trade in Western Asia. Magdala is the place to buy and sell the best cloth and dyes, as well as many other items for trade.

Magdala was always crowded. Merchants from all around and far away came there to trade. The merchant ships and caravans all traveled through Magdala.

The person I always contacted to arrange for the trade of my goods was a woman named Mary.

Mary was a very wealthy woman who owned the biggest and best facility for handling the shipment and distribution of dye and cloth.

Lydia had introduced us to Mary. Mary often came to us because she had the means to travel. She was a little older than I, and very beautiful when she was not suffering from one of her "spells".

I had known her for a while before I saw her in this terrible condition. She would be dreadfully sad, wringing her hands, and weeping for no apparent reason. Sometimes she would stay in her room, and refuse to see anyone at all.

It often caused her to lose customers, and people talked about her behind her back. They said she had devils that made her do strange things. I even heard that she would also try to harm herself.

Zilla was a great help to me as we dealt with Mary. Other people had treated Zilla badly before she had her encounter with Jesus, so Zilla had great compassion for people, especially women, who were suffering in any way.

Because of Zilla, I tried to have patience and wait for Mary to calm down. She always returned to normal in a day or so, but the time in between was often extremely bad.

When Zilla overheard some others say that Mary was demon possessed, Zilla immediately wanted to tell Jesus. Zilla knew that Jesus had cast demons out of several people. She was certain he could help Mary as well.

Thank goodness for Zilla's faith, I honestly, was so scared of doing something to upset Mary that I did not even think about telling Jesus. Zilla got her wish sooner than any of us would have thought.

We had packed up our goods, our clothes, and provisions for the trip, and along with our guard and servants, we prepared to join a caravan heading for the Sea of Galilee.

It was about 80 miles from Magdala to Jerusalem. The trip would take a few days. Zilla was excited about going, but honestly, I would have preferred to stay at home.

I think I may have met my match in Zilla, even Martha agreed that she had more energy and audacity than I did.

The trip seemed longer than usual, but finally we could see the hills and at last, the pass that would take us to our destination.

Mary, the indigo merchant had arranged for us to stay in her home for the 10 days we would be there.

Thank goodness, Mary was in a good mood, and the unpacking went without incident. We got a good price for our dye and the purple cloth that the women in Bethel and surrounding towns had woven.

It was the last full day of our stay. We were getting ready to pack and leave the next day.

Zilla and I had gotten up early. We had gone to supervise the packing of the camels and donkeys for the trip home. I had purchased scarlet thread, and other things that we were taking back as gifts.

It was about time for lunch when we heard a familiar voice calling our names, "Mary, Zilla, what are you doing here?"

It was Peter and the other disciples! Jesus was with them too. We invited them to share our meal.

They had much to tell us about their travels and the wonderful things that had happened while they had been away.

Just as we were about to get settled for our meal, we heard a piercing scream coming from Mary's work place.

Several of the disciples ran to see if they could help, and about that time, Mary came screaming and running out of the building!

She was so distraught that I thought someone was chasing her. There was no one else there except her trusted servant, Heshel, who was trailing after her.

I had heard of these fits, but had never seen Mary like this. It was scary! I realized why others had said she was demon possessed.

As soon as Jesus saw Mary, he stood up and approached her. She threw herself down on the ground at his feet! He began to call names, and tell those beings to leave her.

"Loose her!" he said.

He did this several times, calling different names. When he was finished, Mary lay at his feet as if she was asleep. Jesus touched her gently on her back; she opened her eyes and looked at him. She was calm, and her eyes were clear.

He took her by the hand and helped her up. He said, "Mary, you are free. The power of God has delivered you."

We were all astounded! Zilla was ecstatic! She knew that Mary's personal demons were gone for good.

Mary did too! I have never seen anyone so grateful in my life. She wept for joy. She hugged Jesus right there in the street!

That began a relationship that we all shared for the rest of our lives. Mary turned her business over to trusted servants and relatives, and began to follow Jesus and his disciples wherever they went. She used her wealth to help them pay for food and lodging.

She was known as Mary from Magdalene ever since. Everyone called her Mary Magdalene to distinguish her from Mary, Jesus' mother and myself. Just like the name Jesus, Mary was quite a common name at that time.

Soon after her experience with Jesus and the demons, Mary Magdalene had a beautiful cloak woven from the most beautiful purple cloth she could find. She had the symbols of King David's linage woven into the hem.

Jesus was of the linage of David, so those symbols were his family story. Mary presented the robe to Jesus, and he wore it to the very end.

We spent many happy hours with Mary in our home. She often stayed with us when Jesus and his disciples were in the area. We came to love her like a sister.

CHAPTER 21

MADNESS AND MIRACLES

For the next few months, Jesus and his followers spent most of their time in and around Galilee.

I guess it is hard to think of the boy who grew up a carpenter's son, a boy who attended synagogue with you, as anyone that special. Because of all that, the men of Nazareth refused to accept Jesus' teaching.

It is quite a journey from Bethel to Galilee, and Lazarus was often sick during that time, so we did not travel too far away from home.

I still wondered why Jesus had not healed Lazarus. He seemed to heal every other sick person he encountered.

I was a little disappointed about that. Jesus said to me that I should have more faith. Well, this did not help my feelings one bit! I had faith that he could heal Lazarus. I had seen Jesus make Lazarus better many times, but Lazarus continued to get sick repeatedly. I knew Jesus could heal Lazarus so that he would never be sick again. How much more faith did I need?

We heard many tales of the things Jesus and his many followers were doing while they were traveling around.

We heard of many people healed, wonderful stories that Jesus would tell to illustrate his teaching, we even heard about Peter and Jesus walking on water.

That one was hard to believe, but I heard it from Peter himself. He was so excited that there was no way I could not believe him.

Things were getting even harder for Jews now. King Herod Antipas was living with his brother's wife, Herodias. This was definitely against our laws, but I guess if you are King, you can do whatever you please.

Of course, no one would speak out against Herod because he would have had those persons arrested. Jesus' cousin John was one of those whom Herod had arrested.

We had not seen Jesus and his followers in about six months. So, we were happy to see Peter and Andrew when they came to stay a few days with us.

They told us that Jesus had sent them out to teach the Jews, and tell them about the Kingdom of God. They said Jesus had told them to go to the lost sheep of Israel. To heal, cast out evil spirits, and tell them that the kingdom of heaven was near.

He told them not go to any of the Gentiles or go near the towns of the Samaritans.

I wondered why Jesus had excluded those people. Peter said he did too, but he knew better than to question Jesus.

They were to take nothing with them except the clothes on their backs, and they were to stay with the people who would show them kindness, and invite them in.

Jesus also told the disciples that if anyone treated them badly, they were to leave that place and not return. God would bless those who helped them, and it would be bad for the ones who did not.

Wonderful things had happened to them during that time, and they were not the same men we had known before. They were bold and excited about the power of God that they had received.

We were enjoying their company up until we got the terrible news about Jesus' cousin John. Herod had executed John!

Evidently, Herod's so-called wife, Herodias, had plotted to have John killed. She hated John because he dared to tell the truth about her and Herod living together even though she was still the wife of Herod's brother.

Herod was the most gullible man I had ever seen. His biggest problem was his desire for women.

Several months after John had been arrested; Herod staged a huge party for some of the men who were important political leaders.

Herodias had persuaded him to let her beautiful daughter, Salome, dance for the king and his guests.

That evil queen then told Salome to wear multiple veils and no clothes under them. Herodias instructed her to tease Herod with these semi-transparent veils by taking them off one by one until she got nearly naked.

Before she removed the last veil, she was to ask him for a gift with the promise that she would take all of the veils off.

The men had been eating and drinking for some time before Herodias sent Salome into the banquet hall. Most of the guests were inebriated by the time Salome entered the room.

The dance went just as Herodias had planned. Herod was ready to give that girl anything if she would get naked before them all.

She had one last veil to remove. That wise young woman said, 'What will you give me now, if I remove this last veil?"

Herod answered, "Name anything you want, up to half my kingdom!"

I could not believe such a foolish man was leading our people. Of course, the cunning girl went to her mother to see what she should ask for, and Herodias said, "Ask for John the Baptist's head on a silver platter."

I must say, I think I could have come up with my own request, and it surely would not have been a bloody head on a platter.

It broke my heart when I heard how foolish and cruel this was. I knew it was also going to break Jesus' heart. I was so very sad.

I also learned that this particular request sobered Herod up in a hurry. He was about half-afraid of John to begin with. John's preaching had made him think of his own sin. Herod had also been secretly having John brought to him so he could ask John questions about spiritual things.

This put Herod on the spot. On the one hand, he did not want to kill John, but he had given his word in front of all those witnesses. He felt forced to give Salome what she asked.

He immediately sent an executioner to kill John, and that awful woman got what she wanted. I will always think that Salome felt betrayed by her mother.

We were all heartbroken. Jesus tried to get away for a few days with his disciples after that.

We found out later, that when they tried to go to the sea, the crowds saw them get into Peter's boat. The people were waiting on the opposite shore when the boat arrived.

Instead of trying to avoid them, Jesus sat down to teach once more, and a most remarkable thing happened. One of our neighbors who was there told us about it. He was so astounded that he had hurried back home as fast as his poor donkey could go. He wanted to tell everyone the astounding news!

Jesus had sat on a big outcropping of stone near the shore, and taught the people many things about the kingdom of heaven, he had healed many sick people, and many of them believed that He was the promised Messiah.

It had gotten late, and most of those people had not eaten all day. One of Jesus' disciples said to him, "These people need to leave, and go buy food. Send them away so we can eat also."

About that time, Peter's brother Andrew said, "Here is a boy with five little barley loaves and two fish, but that won't go very far in this multitude."

Jesus did a most extraordinary thing. He told everyone to sit down; He took that little boy's food, and prayed a blessing over it. Then he divided the loves and fish among the

disciples, and asked them to start passing out the food.

Every time they gave food to someone, there was more in the basket.

There were nearly ten thousand people there that day! All the men, women and children ate as much as they wanted, and afterward, the disciples picked up twelve baskets of leftover fish and bread.

Everyone in Judea heard about this miracle. It stirred up more opposition to Jesus' ministry, because the Chief Priests and Pharisees were afraid that he would gain more power over the people than they had. I secretly hoped that he would! Just think what five thousand armed men could do.

Chapter 22

The Centurion Again

Ever since the day when Jesus made that little boy's lunch feed thousands of people, the religious rulers, Pharisees and Sadducees, began planning how they could diminish Jesus' influence over the common people.

I think they were jealous because they could not perform miracles when they taught. However, more than that, I think they feared Jesus' power. They knew the prophecies of the Messiah. I believe they saw what Jesus did, and feared for their own power over the people. They also wanted to keep the favor they had gained under the Romans.

About this time, the Centurion, who had saved me that day in my field, entered the picture again. I heard the story from Mary Magdalene, who was there when it happened.

She said that Jesus had just returned to Capernaum, and as he was walking into town with his disciples, a group of Jewish leaders approached him.

They said a certain centurion named Gavius had a very valuable and trusted slave who was sick.

The slave was near death. The Jewish elders in the town said, "This Roman is a good man, he has helped us often. He even helped build the synagogue here."

That did not surprise me much, because I had been witness to his compassion.

The centurion had begged them to see if Jesus would heal the servant. Jesus said, "Yes. Take me to him."

They were almost to the home of the captain, when some more people met them and said to them, "Gavius has said please don't go all this way. I understand that you are tired and busy. All I ask is that you say the words to heal my servant and I know it will happen. Just like when I give an order and it is done, I know all you have to do is speak the word and it will also be done."

Mary said that Jesus had been amazed at the man's faith. Jesus stopped and spoke to the people who had followed him. They were hoping to see another miracle. Instead, He said, "I have not seen this kind of trust in any of you who should know the scriptures, and should also understand how God can work."

The messengers of the centurion went home, and found the servant out of his bed and well!

I was so happy to hear that Gavius trusted Jesus, and he was helping the Jews in the city.

It cheered me to know that not all Romans were bad. There would be other encounters with

Gavius sooner than I would have imagined and I never could have dreamed where and how.

Chapter 23

A Talk with Jesus' Mother

I was almost certain that Jesus was the long-awaited Messiah, but I wanted some sort of proof. I had always been stubborn. I needed to see for myself if a thing was true or not. In certain ways that was good. It kept me out of trouble quite often.

This time I decided to have a talk with Jesus' mother, Mary. She had moved in with Peter and his wife. This was a good arrangement because Peter was gone a lot and the two Mary's could be of help to each other.

Mary's husband, Joseph, had died when Jesus was just starting to study with the Essenes. Jesus' brothers and sisters were all married and living near Galilee, so Peter's home was a safe place for Mary.

I made the trip to Bethsaida with Zilla. We took the donkeys, Lucifer and Eli, to carry our belongings and gifts for Mary. I had sent word ahead that we were coming.

All of us were dusty and tired when we arrived. A servant helped us unload the donkeys, and get them settled in a shelter nearby. He then showed us to our room so we could wash away the dust of our trip.

Mary was waiting for us with a table set with bread, figs, cheese, and wine. We were so happy to see her, and more than ready for the food.

After we caught up on the news of Mary and our friends, we presented our gifts of purple cloth and sweet lavender oil from my garden. I asked Mary to tell us about Jesus' birth and the early years when he was a boy.

"Mary, will you tell us about when Jesus was born. You know we have heard all the rumors, but I know you can tell us what the real story is."

She told Zilla and myself the entire story. By now, you have probably heard it too. Many others have written the story in their accounts of Jesus' life, but I heard it straight from Jesus' mother.

She told us that she was a virgin when Jesus was born. The Holy Spirit of God had placed Jesus in her womb. The Archangel Gabriel visited her. He told her that God had chosen her to be the mother of His own son!

Mary did not have relations with Joseph until over a year after Jesus was born. Joseph must have been a very good man also.

Mary said that he had been wondering if he should quietly send her away to some safe place.

Mary could have been stoned to death for having a baby when she was not married.

An Angel visited Joseph too. The angel told him that Mary was going to be the mother of God's Son and Joseph should not worry about what other people might say about them.

The people in Nazareth had talked about her, and Mary said it made her sad, mostly because she felt bad for Joseph. She loved him very much.

I could certainly see why. It took great courage to protect Mary. Many people believed that the baby was not his. Joseph kept quiet about it, and always protected Mary and Jesus.

She even told me about the trip to Bethlehem when she was almost ready to deliver the baby and how painful that was.

Here is the story Mary told to us:

It was during the time when Caesar Augustus had ordered everyone to return to the city of his or her family lineage to register.

We knew he was going to levy more taxes, and he was making sure no one would get out of paying.

Both Joseph and I were of the linage of David, so I had to accompany Joseph when he went to Bethlehem, the city of our ancestors.

While we were on that journey, Joseph recalled words from the prophet Micah.

Micah had said, 'But you, Bethlehem Ephrathah, though you were small among the clans of Judah, out *of you will come for me one who will be ruler over Israel whose origins are from of old, from ancient times.'* [8]

We had always been told that this prophesy was about the Messiah." I will never forget what Joseph had said next.

Joseph said, "Mary, do you realize that you must be going to deliver your child on this journey. We both know this child is the Messiah we have prayed for."

It was a hard journey, but Mary said she knew they would make it to Bethlehem safely. What she did not expect was that there would be no place in the city to stay.

Mary went on to say that Joseph was terrified that the baby would be born in the street. She was beginning to worry too, when they came to the last place in town that might provide a space. "No room", the owner had said. As Mary told it, Joseph said, "But my wife is in labor! She is nearing the time to deliver! Surly you can find someplace for her."

That poor innkeeper thought a moment, and then he said, "There is a dry cave where I keep the animals. You could go there."

Mary told us, "I would have gladly gone anywhere it was dry. We found the place and, sure enough, it was dry but there was a donkey,

---

8 Micah 5:2

a cow, three sheep, and chickens in there as well.

By this time the baby was about to come, no matter where we were." She said that Joseph found some dry straw in the back of the little cave. He laid his cloak down for her, and in no time, Jesus was born.

Joseph had made a bed in the feed trough for the baby with more straw.

"That was not how I had dreamed the Son of God would be born." Mary's eyes sparkled as she told that part.

We wondered why Jesus had never told us about how he was born. (Maybe because none of us had thought to ask.)

Mary also told us about shepherds that had showed up the next day, and she said these men had told her and Joseph about the angels in the night sky.

Then I recalled the story that Papa had told us all those years ago. It must have been our friend Jesus in Papa's story. I was astounded!

Mary even told us how those shepherds had found She, Joseph and Jesus in that cave, and had actually bowed down to worship Jesus.

She said she and Joseph had to stay in Bethlehem for seven more days, because they still had to register with the government.

The circumcision of Jesus was required on the eighth day after his birth. Mary was also required to make a sacrifice for her own purity after giving birth. All these things required the offering of a sacrifice at the temple in Jerusalem.

Since Bethlehem was only six miles from the Holy City, and the journey back to Nazareth would take too long, it seemed better to stay in Bethlehem.

Mary confirmed what our father had told us about the old priest and the Holy woman in the temple that day. The baby was Jesus, but father could not have possibly known who the baby was when he told the story to us.

Mary seemed so happy that I had asked her to tell the story. She said she had not told many people because no one would have believed it all.

I knew for sure after our visit that Jesus was God's son. He was the long-awaited Messiah. Zilla was not in the least surprised.

Zilla and I stayed with Jesus' mother for several days. She told us many wonderful stories about Jesus and the other children that she and Joseph had raised together.

Mary told us that Jesus had learned Joseph's trade. Jesus and his brothers had helped Joseph with his work. She said Jesus was very talented, seemed to enjoy the work, and never complained; no matter how long or hard the job was.

It was finally time for us to go back home. As we made the trip back to Bethany, I was so excited, and a little scared too. We could not wait to tell Martha and Lazarus all that we had learned.

Lazarus had not been well, so he had not gone with us to see Mary. We knew the dust and length of the trip would have been very bad for him, so he stayed at home. Martha had stayed there to care for him.

It was his breathing again. We needed Jesus to come soon and help him once more. I was still upset that Jesus did not seem concerned about Lazarus. His health had been getting worse all year. I think Jesus was aware of it too.

Jesus was healing people, making the blind men see, and casting demons out of men and women. Why did he not heal Lazarus completely? Was it something we had done? Was it sin in our lives? Had Lazarus done something I did not know about?

It would be a while, but I would have the answers to all those questions.

CHAPTER 24

PREPARING THE DISCIPLES

Jesus was becoming more and more popular with the common people. Huge crowds were following him everywhere he went. It was hard for him to have time to eat, not to mention having any time alone.

Many, like us, believed he was the Messiah that God had promised. There was great excitement among the people, but the chief priests and scribes were still not happy about him.

I could not understand this at all. Surely, they wanted freedom from our oppressors. I knew they heard him preach, saw the demons cast out, and lepers healed…not since the completion of the Torah had a Jewish leper been healed.

After all, it was against the rules because Lepers are unclean according to the laws. We knew we could get leprosy through skin contact. People would not touch a leper, fearing they would get the disease. None of that mattered to Jesus. I suppose He had faith that God would protect him.

The only thing I could figure out was that the temple rulers loved their power over the people more than they wanted God's plan.

If Jesus became King of the Jews, those men would no longer be in charge.

That was pretty silly because they only had as much power as Rome would allow, and all of us knew that any one of them could lose it all if Caesar wanted to take them out.

Some other people believed, but wanted more signs that Jesus was indeed the King God had promised.

We even heard that some of the Pharisees and Sadducees had gathered around Jesus one day as he was teaching, and asked him for a sign. They wanted to know for sure if he was the Messiah.

It seemed to upset Jesus so very much that they wanted another sign. He told them that the only sign they would get would be the sign of Jonah.

We were as confused about what he meant as they were. We believed, because we knew that he had powers no one had ever seen or heard of before. What in the world was the sign of Jonah? Was a whale going to gobble up these unbelieving men? Would they all die? What could happen in three days that would be like Jonah? It was quite a mystery.

Jesus gathered twelve of his most faithful followers, and set them apart to be a sort of "inner group". He began to teach these twelve more about doing God's Will.

It was almost as if Jesus was getting ready to send them out to help spread the word about God's plan for His kingdom.

As I look back, that was exactly what he was doing, but it would not happen when, and certainly not how, any of us would have ever imagined.

After a short trip through Caesarea, the disciples all headed back to Galilee. It was time for the feast of Tabernacles.

All Jewish men are required to attend this feast. Lazarus was barely able to attend because he was growing much weaker. Even the short journey from our home to Jerusalem was hard for him.

He was only able to attend the feast because of the generosity of Mary from Magdala. She hired a litter for him to ride in. I am sure that was quite a surprise for many, because rarely, did Jews have that luxury.

We knew that Jesus' brothers were going to the feast, and his disciples, but none of them thought that Jesus would come. It was getting dangerous for him in Jerusalem.

Some of the religious leaders believed he was guilty of blasphemy, while others were waiting for him to declare himself king of the Jews.

Many of his followers were ready to fight for that cause!

They were certain that if they were to start the rebellion, Jesus had the miraculous power to overthrow the Romans, as well as any Jews who would stand in his way.

There was lots of talk about a rebellion in the secret meetings held in some Jewish homes. There were even meetings in a few synagogues also.

I would have gladly helped them in any way I could if it came to a fight!

Jews, especially women, faced death nearly every day we lived among the Romans. We never knew when one of those Romans might decide to make an example of us. If I was going to die, I wanted it to be for a cause worthy of my life.

Jesus did go to the feast, but he went alone, and showed up about three days into the seven-day feast.

As usual, the crowds gathered around him. Lazarus said that he spoke out plainly, and accused some of the men of trying to kill him.

Many in the crowd angrily accused Jesus of being demon possessed, and they got angry, and really did try to kill him.

Lazarus said it was as if he had some supernatural protection, and no one was able to touch him.

The Temple rulers tried to send guards to arrest Jesus, but the guards heard what Jesus was saying. Jesus' teaching so impressed them that they did not lay a hand on him.

Of course, this did not help Jesus' popularity with the Pharisees and Sadducees at all. This may be when they began to plot to get Jesus out of their hair for good.

CHAPTER 25

We had seen Jesus only once since the Feast of Tabernacles. He visited briefly before the Feast of the Temple Dedication in December. Lazarus had been getting weaker by the day, but he was very glad to see Jesus when Jesus came to see us after the feast.

Jesus laid his hands on Lazarus' chest, and prayed over him. Lazarus felt better while Jesus was here. He even got up and ate with us all. I was very much encouraged.

Jesus and the twelve disciples stayed for a couple of days. While they were here, I observed something that bothered me a lot.

Martha had saved some money from the parties she provided. She wanted to give it to Jesus to help with their travel expenses. Jesus thanked her, and handed the coins to one of the disciples whom I did not know very well.

His name was Judas, and he was from the town of Kerioth. Everyone called him Judas Iscariot, which means the Man from Kerioth in Hebrew.

Anyway, I was watching when Jesus handed the money to Judas.

I saw Judas put most of the money in the pouch he carried, but I also observed that he dropped a few coins into a pocket inside his cloak.

I thought this was strange. I wanted to say something to Jesus about it, but I never had an opportunity to see him alone during that visit.

Jesus and his followers stayed a few days with us, and seemed relaxed and refreshed when they left us to go back to Perea.

Lazarus felt better for a few weeks, but it was not long before he fell deathly ill again. He was so sick that his skin turned a bluish color. He was struggling to breathe.

I prayed to God to send Jesus back. We sent a messenger on the fastest horse we could find to tell Jesus. I knew that Jesus would come, and I thought Lazarus might be able to make it until he got here.

The rider returned, and said Jesus was on his way, but his disciples had caused a delay. They were afraid that the trip would be too dangerous for Jesus, and it took him a while to convince them to come along.

I knew there were people who wanted to kill Jesus, but I also believed that his Father, God, would protect him. After all, how can a dead man become king?

On the day after our messenger returned, Lazarus took a terrible turn for the worse. He was dead by nightfall.

We were devastated! Where in the world was Jesus? I felt betrayed by the one I loved most in the entire world.

I believed that if Jesus had just said the word from wherever he was, he could have healed Lazarus. After all, He had done that for the Centurion. I was sure he could have done it for us too.

All we could do was prepare Lazarus body for burial. It was summer, and we needed to hurry. A body would start to decay quickly in the heat.

All our neighbors, relatives, and friends were there when we laid Lazarus in our family tomb. It was the tomb where we had placed Mama and Papa all those years before.

As was the custom, almost everyone stayed at our house, so we would not be alone in our grief. I was inconsolable! I refused to be comforted, although many were there and they tried to make me feel better.

Four days later word came that Jesus was finally here.

Martha ran out to meet him. I was so upset that I stayed inside the house.

What good was it that he was here now? It had been three days, and by this time and Lazarus' body would have begun to decay. I could hardly stand the thought of that.

Martha met Jesus outside the village near the tomb where we had placed Lazarus' body. Soon she came running into the house and told me that Jesus was asking for me. I knew better than to deny the Messiah, so I went to the burial place where Jesus was waiting.

Many of our guests followed me. That did not make me happy, but I did not say anything to them.

When I reached the place where Jesus was waiting, I could not help myself, I cried out, "Lord, if you had only come sooner Lazarus would not have died"[9].

He looked at me with tears running down his face and asked, "Where have you laid him?"

Everyone followed as Jesus, Martha, and myself went to the family tomb. We could hear the people discussing why Jesus had not come earlier. Most of them believed as we did, that Jesus could have healed Lazarus.

When we all arrived at the tomb, Jesus said, "Roll away the stone."

I was shocked! What was he thinking? In this heat, there would be a horrible odor, no one wanted to see how bad the body would be.

Martha and I tried to warn him, but he said the strangest thing to us. He looked right into my eyes and said, "Didn't I tell you that if you believed, you would see the glory of God?"[10]

---

9 The Narrated Bible p.1434

10 The Narrated Bible p.1435

Then he said to everyone, "Go ahead, and take away the stone." [11] It took several strong men to roll away the stone.

Then Jesus looked up at the sky, and quietly said a prayer to His Father in Heaven, and then he shouted, "Lazarus, Come Out!"

Lazarus walked out of the tomb still wrapped in the grave clothes. I thought I was going to faint!

Jesus ordered the men who had rolled the heavy stone aside to help Lazarus out of the grave clothes. They did, and left only the ones around his most private parts.

Martha and I rushed to embrace our brother, and to get him back to our home. What Joy! After all these years, I still cannot describe it. The memory of that day still makes me want to shout for joy and dance all around!

Nearly everyone who witnessed Lazarus' resurrection believed that Jesus was the Messiah who the scriptures had predicted would come. Everybody was overjoyed. We celebrated for days!

Later we learned that some of the people who were there went to the Pharisees, and told what Jesus had done. I truly do not know if they wanted to prove to those doubting teachers and leaders that Jesus was really the Messiah, or if they meant to harm Jesus. It really does not

---

matter now. What they did set the stage for the terrible things that would happen later.

Those in power sent out the word that if anyone knew where Jesus was, they were to report it to them. We suspected they might try to arrest Jesus so they could question him about his motives.

After that, Jesus and his close followers stayed in Ephraim near the desert. They kept to themselves, and tried to avoid big crowds. Jesus still could not resist healing people, blessing children, trying to convince the few

Pharisees who came around, that it was not all about the law.

He also tried to tell the close followers (Lazarus was there for some of these talks) that it might not end as they all hoped.

Most of us did not understand was about to happen. The next time I saw Jesus was probably the most important evening of my life.

CHAPTER 26

LAZARUS HAS PROOF

We were overjoyed to see Lazarus when he returned home after being with Jesus and his men. I lived in fear of someone trying to kill Lazarus. That would be just like some of those power-hungry Pharisees, or even a few of the Sadducees, to try to kill Lazarus. Then they would say that we had all imagined that Lazarus had risen from the dead. They make up the worst lies, and some people actually fall for them.

Martha was happy to have a reason to cook and scurry around the kitchen. She made a fabulous meal for us all.

As we reclined around the table after the meal, Lazarus began to tell us what he had learned during his last visit with Jesus and his followers.

Lazarus said that Jesus had reminded them about three miracles that only the coming Messiah would do.

These are miracles listed in the books of the Prophets as a way to identify the Messiah. Only the Messiah would be able to perform these feats.

One of these wonders was the healing of a Jewish leper. Our laws label Lepers as unclean

Jews are forbidden to touch a leprous person. The disease is terribly contagious. It can often spread simply by touching a person who has leprosy.

In addition, if a Jew somehow was healed of the disease, that person must immediately present himself, or herself, to the priest, offer a sacrifice, and be questioned by the priest about the healing in order to discover if, indeed, they were actually healed.

Jesus had healed a Jewish Leper, and had sent the man to the Temple to tell the priest. Most everyone knew about that incident and we were sure the priest knew about the ancient prophesy too. No one ever heard what the priest had said or done after the former Leper's confession.

Not only did Jesus heal that one man, but also another time, Jesus healed seven lepers at the once. Only one of them came back to thank Jesus for healing him.

The next prophesied miracle was casting a demon out of a deaf and mute person. The traditional way of exorcising a demon required asking its name, then calling the demon out by name. A deaf person could neither hear the question, nor speak the name of the demon. Jesus did not need to hear the demon's name. He drove the demon out.

The man could both hear and speak afterward. The Jewish tradition says that only the coming Messiah can do that.

Isiah, the prophet, wrote about the third miracle. Isiah said that only the Messiah would be able to heal a person blind from birth. Anyone by the power of God could heal someone who had become blind, but only the Messiah would be able heal a person who had been born blind.

Jesus had healed a man, whom everyone knew, had been blind from birth. Even the priests had questioned that man, and the man had told them that Jesus was the one who had healed his eyes.

We were more convinced than ever that Jesus was the true Messiah, and we realized that the Sadducees and Pharisees must have known it too. They all knew the words of the Prophets better than anyone else.

We were astounded to think that these men would try to reject the Messiah of God. Surely, God would strike them down. There was no way that they did not know who Jesus really was. I was sure if they would help him, Jesus would find places for them in his kingdom. Oh, how wrong I was.

Later, after Lazarus had told us about his visit with Jesus and his disciples, I asked him something that had been on my mind for days.

"Lazarus, I want to know what heaven is like. What happened after you died, and before Jesus raised you back to life?"

"I wondered if you were ever going to ask," Lazarus said. "It felt like I had fallen asleep, and had suddenly awakened in a new place. It was warm, and there was a golden glow all around."

"I felt so peaceful and safe. A tall beautiful creature was there. I knew it was an angel. I felt no fear, but I was amazed and in awe of that being. The Angel told me that I was not going into heaven now, but I would someday return."

"The angel said that Jesus still had work on earth for me, and Jesus would call me back to earth soon."

"It seemed like only a moment had passed before I heard Jesus' voice calling to me. I turned to look, I was in the tomb, the stone was rolling away and Jesus was calling for me to come out."

I must admit, I was a little bit jealous of Lazarus' experience. I would love to see an angel!

Lazarus never mentioned this again to us, but he was different. He had a peace that I could only wish for, and as far as I know, he was not afraid of anything after that.

CHAPTER 27

AN EVENING WITH THE KING

Martha was helping with a big banquet at Simon the Leper's house. Simon was the man that Jesus had healed of leprosy. Lazarus was invited, and I had a plan to attend too; no one knew that but me.

Somehow, I had known that it was time for me to take the alabaster jar of Spikenard from its hiding place.

I removed the jar from its place in my room. How could I have forgotten how beautiful it was?

I remembered that beautiful day with Jesus in my garden. So much has happened since then. I must admit that I had taken the jar out a few times over the years, and wondered what I might do with it. I imagined selling it, and giving the money to Jesus when the revolt to overturn the Romans would start.

This time I knew for sure why Jesus gave the oil to me. This oil was not to fund the revolt. It was time to anoint a king!

I took the jar of oil with me to Simon's house. Everyone was finishing the meal. Martha had received much deserved praise for the food and the hospitality.

As she and her helpers were starting to clear away the food and utensils, I slipped into the room with the jar of Spikenard. I thought I would be anointing an earthly king, but actually, it would be something entirely different.

I tiptoed quietly over and knelt at Jesus' feet. I looked up into his face. He gave me the sweetest smile, and whispered, "Go ahead, Mary. This is the reason I gave this gift to you all those years ago. "

I removed the covering from my head. I let my hair loose. My hair was long; it reached almost to my knees. I knelt in front of Jesus. I anointed his feet and gently poured some of the oil into his head. I carefully washed it the excess off with my own hair.

The wonderful fragrance of that precious oil filled the whole room.

If I live to be one hundred years old, I will never forget the loving look that Jesus gave me. That look will stay burned into my memory forever.

I was sure that Jesus would claim his authority now. I thought I was ready for whatever would come next. What happened after I put the vial away was a little strange.

Judas got very indignant. He said, "This is an outrage! That oil could have been sold, and the money used to feed many poor people!"

I knew that he would have sold it all right, but the money would have never gone anywhere but into his own pocket. He almost ruined my beautiful moment with Jesus.

I did not quite understand it then, but I will forever remember what Jesus said to him.

"Leave her alone," he said, "It was intended that she should save this perfume for the day of my burial."

"You will always have the poor among you, but you will not always have me. I tell you the truth, wherever the gospel is preached throughout the world, what she has done will also be told, in memory of her."[12]

The day of his burial? What did he mean? I wondered too about the things he said about me.

I was not sure what to do next. Jesus leaned over and whispered in my ear, "Mary, God will bless you in ways you will not expect for this act of love"

My heart skipped a beat at his words. I did not remember what he had said about his burial until much later.

I could find no words to say, I kissed the top of Jesus' head, took the empty jar, covered my hair, and quietly left the room. I knew I would have to answer to Martha later about the Spikenard.

I got out just in time. A large group of people came into the room. They had heard that Jesus and Lazarus were both there.

Poor Lazarus had not been able to go anywhere without crowds wanting to see and touch him. I believe those people needed to see, as well as touch Lazarus in order to prove to themselves that Lazarus was truly alive.

Many people began to believe that Jesus was the Messiah, and were following him because of what he had done for Lazarus.

As for Martha, she never did mention the oil to me. I believe that she too, understood the significance of my love for Jesus. Several weeks later, I told her the whole story. By then she was not at all surprised.

We have kept that jar all these years as a reminder of the joyful memories we have of Jesus and the times he spent with us.

We had heard rumors that during this Passover week, insurgents were going to try to force Jesus into declaring himself King.

I too, figured we might have to do something to force the issue. Jesus did not seem to be in any hurry to claim his place of authority. We also knew there would probably be a fight.

With God on our side, how could we possibly fail? We were getting excited. Passover was only a few days away.

CHAPTER 28

CAN YOU FIND A DONKEY?

It was the week of Passover. Jesus and a few of his disciples were staying with us for a few days. The others were also in Bethel, but in the homes of other friends.

Lazarus told us that many people who had been following Jesus were going to declare him King during Passover week.

As far as we knew, Jesus was unaware of this plot. The people thought he would not refuse once he saw how many were willing to help him.

The plan would be for the people to declare Jesus king right before Passover. Of course, they were ready to fight; they knew that no one in power was going to agree to this demand. Many had be storing up weapons in preparation for the battle.

I thought it might be better if Jesus knew about all this, but I kept my thoughts to myself. Not one of them would have listened, even if I could have figured out whom to tell. I was very concerned.

All the men wanted to go into Jerusalem. Martha, Zilla and I followed along. Just as we approached the edge of Bethany, we saw two of Jesus' disciples untying a colt from a post.

The owner came out and asked what they were doing.

Seriously! I wondered about that myself. The men simply said, "The Master needs the colt."

Well, I was surprised when the man said, "Take them both; the colt will not want to go without its mother."

We followed along as they took the two animals to the place where Jesus had been waiting.

The men began to get the colt ready for Jesus to ride. I wondered why he did not ride the mother donkey, but he was adamant that the unridden colt was the one he wanted to ride.

One of the disciples took off his own cloak, and put it on the colt's back. That little donkey stood there as if it had ridden every day.

I was astounded! I was also more than a little concerned. Jesus usually walked, so why did he need the donkey. The walk was not a long one. Was he ill or was there another reason?

We went on ahead of them, along with many other people who were also on the way to choose a lamb.

It was lamb selection day, and we all were looking for a perfect male lamb, one without any blemishes. There was a large crowd of people also going to shop.

There were shepherds herding the lambs for sale. All sorts of other people were going into the city as well.

What a commotion! We joined the throng. As always, it was slow going. We had almost gotten to the city gates when we heard people singing. Nearly everyone who was on the way stopped to see what was happening behind us, even the lambs seemed curious.

There was Jesus on the colt, and people were laying their cloaks down in the path before him. Others had broken off palm branches and were covering the path with them. It was as if they were welcoming a king, and I guess they were.

Jesus was wearing the beautiful robe that Mary Magdalene had given him, and he certainly looked like a king.

He even smelled like a king. Part of Jewish the tradition of welcoming a new king involves anointing the new king with expensive oils like the one I used a few days earlier to anoint Jesus' head and feet. That wonderful perfume still filled the air around Jesus.

This was it! There was no way that anyone could miss this sign. Passover was only few days away.

The people were shouting, "Hosanna! Blessed is the one who comes in the name of the Lord! Peace in heaven and glory in the highest!"[13]

Then Jesus did the strangest thing. He actually began to weep. John heard him say, "Oh, Jerusalem, if you had only known what would bring you peace!" But now it will be hidden from you"[14] John also said that Jesus had said that Jerusalem would one day be destroyed and not one stone would be left standing.

I never did understand what Jesus said about Jerusalem, but I did not think about it much. I tried to put that kind of thoughts out of my mind. There was so much joy that day! I wanted to enjoy the coming festival, and not think about something about which I could do nothing.

We still had to purchase our lamb for the sacrifice. After Father died, we began buying a lamb instead of raising sheep.

I had enough to do tending the Indigo, Lazarus was busy with the family business and Martha never was much help with animals. Still, we were required to tend the purchased lamb for four days before sacrificing it. That was the law.

This requirement was always troubling for me because I love little creatures. I had always fallen in love with the little lambs, even if we

---

13 Luke 19: 38 NIV Study Bible

14 Luke 19:41-44

only had them for a few days. It broke my heart to see them die.

I guess that is the point though, if we did not have sin in our lives, we would not need a sacrifice to take the sin away – even though we know we will sin again, and have to repeat it all over next year. What a mess Adam and Eve created!

CHAPTER 28

OUR PASSOVER LAMB

We made our way into the market. Martha was worried that we would not find a perfect lamb for our sacrifice. Our plan had been to get there before the market got crowded, but here we were in the middle of the throng. Everyone else was looking for a lamb too.

Lazarus was very adept at getting a bargain from the merchants, so we stood back while he went to several stalls in the animal section of the market. He finally found a lamb that looked like the best one.

Then the bargaining began. We all loved the challenge of making the best deal – both merchant and buyer. The merchant quoted an exorbitant price, Lazarus made a counter offer. This went on for quite a while before Martha gave her nod of approval, and Lazarus agreed to the final price.

We had just finished that purchase, and were about to go out to shop into the rest of the market. All of a sudden, we heard a big uproar coming from the Temple Court of The Gentiles. This was where the temple officials rented booths to merchants. They charged a tax plus a big fee for the privilege.

We heard Tables crashing, people yelling, saw animals running everywhere and birds flying in all directions! We stopped in our tracks, not sure which way was best to get out of the way.

Lazarus had the lamb. It was struggling to get loose, and we were trying to get out of there too.

In the middle of all this mayhem was Jesus. He was angry, and shouting! I had never seen him like this – ever. He was turning over tables, scattering money and animals all over the place. I heard him say, "Is it not written in the Torah My house will be called a house of prayer for all nations? But you have made it a den of thieves!"[15]

The other people who were shopping seemed to agree, after all, the merchants charged outrageous prices, and the Pharisees made a bunch of money on things that should have been holy.

We could tell the rulers were mad. However, they were scared of all the people who were following, and listening to Jesus. Maybe his time had finally come. In the middle of all that commotion, I could have sworn that I saw Judas sneak away into the temple.

I wondered what business Judas had in the inner courts.

I thought he was probably up to no good. Maybe he was trying to make a deal to sell

---

15 Isaiah 56:7 Jer. 7:11 The Narrated Bible

something to some greedy Pharisee. It is just as well that I did not know, because if I had known the truth then, I probably would have messed up the whole plan for Jesus.

We finally made our way out of Jerusalem. It was good to be safely on the road toward our house. The little lamb seemed to calm down, and so did we. The next day was Sabbath. We needed to get home.

CHAPTER 30

PREPARING FOR THE FEAST

By this time, most of the big crowds that had been following Jesus were busy with their own preparations. Jesus and the twelve faithful followers wanted to visit the temple, and then spend some time together on the Mt of Olives.

That little garden is on a hill near our town. It had always been one of Jesus' favorite spots. It is full of ancient olive trees. These trees are all twisted and knotty but still bore delicious fruit. I am sure he and his friends had eaten the fruit often. It was not olive season now, but the trees provide shelter and shade in all seasons. The garden is a good place to sit, talk and even pray.

Jesus and I have this in common, we both feel close to God in a garden. The whole city of Jerusalem is visible from this particular garden. Jesus and the disciples have spent the night there many times in the last few years.

Peter told us not to expect them to stay with us on Tuesday night. Jesus had sent them to a place in Jerusalem where they were going to prepare for the Passover meal.

I had stayed home to clean the leaven from our home, and prepare for our own feast.

Peter told us later that Jesus had sent himself and John to a place to help prepare for the meal.

They had no idea when or how Jesus had arranged for the room, but they were getting used to surprises.

Jesus had told them to follow a man carrying a water jug as they entered the city gate. They were to follow him to a house that he would enter. They were to say to the owner of the house, "The Teacher asks: Where is the guest room, where I may eat the Passover with my disciples?"[16]

They did as Jesus told them. Sure enough, that man led them to the house, and to a room that was on the upper floor. They told us later that they were not even surprised. They were getting used to what we all called "Jesus moments."

There was plenty of space in that room of the house; it was actually a separate living space on the upper floor. They all began to get everything ready for Martha and some of the other women who followed Jesus. The women were coming to help prepare their meal.

Peter said, "Everything went bad after that!"

He said he would never forget the things that followed. It is still so very painful even after all these years.

---

16 The Narrated Bible page 1357

I, too, know how it ended, but my heart still aches to remember the horrible pain, fear, and disbelief at what was about to happen.

Peter said they were all ready. The room was clean, the unleavened bread and wine were ready for the start of Passover. They had removed all the leaven in the house. Our law required the removal of all yeast from every home.

No one could work on a Sabbath either. Passover is a Holy Sabbath even though it did not fall on the actual Sabbath day of that particular week.

The men expected that Jesus would want to celebrate Passover the following day. Still they would have to eat unleavened bread on this night too, because the room was already prepared for Sabbath.

Peter wondered if maybe Jesus would again take them to sleep under the stars on the Mount of Olives after the meal.

It would not be the first time they had slept under those stars this week.

They would wait until Jesus and the others got there to figure that out.

The women; Martha, Mary Magdalene and others did not seem to be too concerned about all these things. They had gotten a meal ready for everyone.

As it turned out, they never got around to eating everything that the women had prepared.

Instead, Jesus and the other men arrived at dusk. Jesus had them all sit down and prepare to eat. Jesus asked for the bread and the wine first. It was almost as if they were going to observe the Passover Feast. Mary gave him what he asked for.

Peter said this had surprised him, but Jesus had astonished them many times before. They were beginning to get used to overlooking Jewish traditions.

Jesus blessed the bread; they ate the bread and drank the four cups of wine required in the Passover ritual. It was not until days later that all of them realized the true significance of that last meal.

Another strange thing that happened right after the wine was finished; Jesus got up, took off his robe, and asked Martha for a basin of water.

He knelt in front of his disciples, and began to wash their feet. Martha felt bad that she had not thought to do that for them all. There was not a servant present to do it when they arrived and, in her preoccupation with the meal, she never even thought to do it herself.

When Jesus came to Peter to wash his feet, Peter was very much distraught.

Martha remembered that Peter had exclaimed, "No Lord, you shall never wash my feet!"

However, Jesus said to Peter, "Unless I wash you, you have no part with me." And Peter had replied, "Then, Lord, not just my feet but my hands and my head as well!"

Then Jesus said, "A person who has had a bath needs only to wash his feet, his whole body is clean. And you are clean, Peter, though not every one of you is clean." [17]

There was much discussion about who was not clean and why. In the mist of the discussion, Jesus said to Judas, "What you are about to do, do quickly." Judas got up and left the room. [18]

The others wondered why Judas had left. Some said he left to buy the food that they still needed for the Passover feast.

After this happened, Jesus said, "Let's go to the garden, it's getting late, and I want to go there and pray."

It was not the first time Jesus had wanted to pray at the Mount of Olives. The disciples were glad to go with him. They left the women to finish the cleanup.

Martha and her friends tidied up the room, and returned to their homes. Most of them still needed to prepare their own homes for Passover.

---

17 John 13:6-11

18 John 13:27b

CHAPTER 31

ARRESTED!

Many days would pass before we learned what actually had happened that night in the garden of olive trees on the hillside.

We heard parts of the story from several of Jesus' disciples, mostly from Peter, James and John. I will tell it in my own words the way I heard it.

It was late by the time they walked up the hill to the olive grove. Jesus told all of them that they would soon turn their backs on him. He also said something that most of them did not understand.

He quoted the prophet Isaiah who wrote, "I will Strike the shepherd, and the sheep of the flock will be scattered" and then he said, "But after I have risen, I will go ahead of you into Galilee" [19]

There was much argument about turning their backs on him. Peter swore that he would never do that. Jesus told Peter that he would deny that he even knew him that very night before the roosters would crow.

---

19 The Narrated Bible Matthew-John

There is a place on the Mount of Olives called Gethsemane. It is a kind of garden within the garden. A quiet place farther up the hill. A place most visitors to the olive trees do not usually visit. Jesus took Peter, James and John and went there to pray some more. The other disciples waited farther down the hill.

It was getting late and everyone was sleepy. Everyone except Jesus, who seemed to be greatly distressed. He went further into the garden alone.

Peter said they all had tried to stay awake, but they could not. The wine they had with supper was having its effect on them. Peter also said they learned later that Jesus had come back two different times to speak to them, but had found them asleep. Finally, the third time, he woke them up and said, "Wake up, It's almost time. I am about to be betrayed. Get up, I hear them coming"

James said that was when things really got confusing. Judas was coming up the hill, and soldiers were following him. There was a group of officials from the chief priests and some Pharisees too.

James told us that they all wondered if the Romans had arrested Judas, and now the soldiers were coming for the rest of them.

Peter drew his sword, and a couple of others took out their weapons too. John said they were scared, but were willing to die protecting Jesus if they had to.

James said that before anyone could do anything, Judas rushed up to Jesus, and greeted him with a kiss. They thought this was very strange.

They all said they would never forget what Jesus said. He said, "Judas, are you going to betray me with a kiss?"

That is exactly what Judas did. Jesus stepped forward after that kiss, and asked the ones who were with Judas, "Who are you looking for? "

"Jesus of Nazareth" the captain said.

Jesus answered, "I am Jesus."

The disciples said that all the soldiers and officials fell to the ground at Jesus' words.

John said the disciples all thought it was over, and they had won, but Jesus spoke again. "Are you not looking for me, Jesus of Nazareth?"

Then the contingent started forward toward Jesus to arrest him. Peter sprang forward, and cut off the ear of one of the servants of the chief priest.

The rest of the disciples were ready to fight also. Jesus shouted to Peter, "Put down your sword!"

Then Jesus held the severed ear up to the man's head, when he removed his hand, he had restored the man's ear. It was as if it had never happened. No one could believe that the soldiers still arrested him! They carried Jesus away with his hands and feet in chains.

The disciples were terrified that others would be on the way to arrest them also.

"Let's get out of here," someone said, and all of the men scattered.

They all ran in different directions. Some to their homes, and others to homes of friends nearby. A few even went back to the room where they had eaten the meal earlier. Only Peter decided to follow along at a distance to see what was going to happen to Jesus.

He followed as far as he could, but stopped when the soldiers took Jesus into the house of Annas, who was the father- in- law of the current high priest. Annas still had great influence among the religious leaders.

Peter waited in a garden nearby, and many other people were there too. Someone there recognized him as one of Jesus' followers. It was a woman, and she asked Peter if he was a disciple of Jesus.

Peter told her he did not even know who Jesus was. She kept questioning him, and Peter told her three different times that he was not a follower.

Suddenly, the words Jesus spoke to him at supper that very night came back to his mind like an evil spirit.

Jesus had warned Peter that he would deny that he knew him. Not only deny Jesus once, Peter would deny him three times.

Jesus said it would happen before the rooster crowed that very day. Just at that moment, Peter heard a rooster crow somewhere nearby. Peter said he was so ashamed that he fell to the ground and wept.

Chapter 32

Running and Hiding

We had no idea that all these things had happened until very early on the morning of Passover.

Martha had gotten home late that night, and we still had a few chores to do to finish our Passover preparations.

Most of the disciples were afraid that the Romans would try to arrest them too. They all had found places to hide hoping the trouble would soon be over.

I was in my herb garden cutting the bitter herbs for the Passover feast, when I saw a man running up the path to our house.

Mary Magdalene had sent a servant to warn us. She was afraid for Lazarus' safety. The servant was out of breath from running, he was terrified and unable to speak.

I got him into the house, and gave him a cup of water. He was finally able to tell us that the rulers had arrested Jesus.

He said it had happened while they all were on the Mount of Olives. Judas had told the Temple rulers where to find Jesus.

I was not at all surprised. I knew Judas was a crook from the moment I saw him pocket that money that day long ago.

The servant said they had taken Jesus to Annas, then to the chief priest. The chief priest had condemned him to die for blasphemy.

The Chief Priest had then sent him to Pilate for sentencing. Jews could not actually sentence anyone to death without Roman permission. Jesus was in Pilate's court when Mary Magdalene had told the servant to run to tell us.

We all agreed that Lazarus should go to the upstairs rooms where Jesus and his men had eaten the night before. It was safe, and no one would suspect that anyone would be there. A few of the other men were there also.

Lazarus only agreed to do this because Martha and I feared for his life. He told us often that after experiencing death once, he would never be afraid of dying again.

I should have remembered that Jesus commanded angels to watch over our property. No man could have harmed Lazarus there. Fear had taken over, and we all seemed to have lost our minds.

Now that we felt Lazarus was safe, Martha, Zilla and I decided to go into Jerusalem. We had to know what was happening.

We were in such a hurry, and so distraught, that we did not even think about our Passover meal, or the lamb we left behind.

As things turned out, we would never eat that Passover meal. Passovers from that day forward would never be the same for us.

Chapter 33

Insanity Reigns

The roads were crowded with pilgrims still making their way into the city. Most were going to the temple for the sacrifice of the Passover lambs. At three in the afternoon, the sacrificing of the lambs would take place. It took many priests and their helpers to do it all. It was very loud and very bloody.

I always dreaded it, but I understood the significance when I watched that little innocent lamb die for my sins. It broke my heart.

Every year I wished I could be sinless, but every year I continued to do things that I knew were not what God wanted me to do. We had so many laws that it was impossible to obey them all. I wished for a better way.

The Passover lamb's blood was how God saved our ancestors from the death angel all those years ago when we were slaves in Egypt. It was then, and still is today, a symbol of God's protection and salvation.

I was thinking about all those things when we entered the city, and heard the crowd yelling.

It sounded like a riot, and Martha and I held hands. We began watching for safe places to hide just in case.

We looked for a familiar face, but it was not until we got close to the place where Pilate, the governor, held court that we saw Peter and John with Jesus' mother Mary.

We joined them and we all stood close to the edge of a crowd of very angry people.

It was then that I saw Jesus. I almost became physically ill at the sight. Peter had to hold me up for a moment. I do not know how Jesus' mother was able to watch.

Those guards had beaten Jesus beyond recognition. They had pushed a thorny wreath onto his head, and blood was running down his head and into his eyes. Blood was running down his chest and his back was bleeding from the slashes that had bared his bones. They had beaten our sweet Jesus to the point of death. I honestly do not know how he had survived.

As we watched, a soldier put Jesus' beautiful robe over his bleeding back. Everyone was making fun of Jesus, and calling him all sorts of names. The soldiers were shouting, "Look at the King of the Jews now!"

Many of the same people who had sung praises just a few days before were now shouting for Jesus' crucifixion. What in the world had happened to these people?

Martha, Mary Magdalene, Jesus' mother, Peter, John and I tried to stay together as the crowd pushed and shoved each other. They continued to shout for Jesus to be crucified. Crucified! That was the punishment for thieves and murderers not an innocent man. I cannot imagine what kind of reason these people had for turning so violent.

I have to say that Pilate tried several times to get the people to accept another way. He offered them a choice between Jesus and a terrorist named Barabbas. It was a custom to set one prisoner free on feast day, and the people could choose.

They screamed ever louder, "Give us Barabbas! Crucify Jesus!" Had the whole world gone mad? I did not want to stay, but my feet felt like they had grown roots, and were anchored into the very ground I where I was standing.

Finally, Pilate had enough; he called for a bowl of water, and washed his hands in front of everyone.

Pilate said, "I'm turning him over to you. I am washing my hands of this whole matter.   I believe you are killing an innocent man."

After the people saw what Pilate had done and heard what he said, they began to shout and call for the crucifixion of Jesus.

The crowd shouted, "Let His blood be on us and on our children! Crucify him!" [20]

This scared me half to death. I said a prayer to God to protect Martha, our little group and I from what they were shouting. They were calling for the death of their Messiah. What would happen to us all? I was terrified!

The guards led Jesus away. Most of the crowd knew they would take him to Golgotha, a mound outside the city wall, where most executions happened.

Golgotha was a particularly gruesome place. Everyone entering Jerusalem had to pass by that spot. What a ghastly way to keep the people intimidated. Bodies and dying people on crosses made everyone think twice before disobeying any of the laws Rome forced on us.

The crowd began to disperse. Some went on with their Passover chores, but many of them followed the procession along the road to the outskirts of Jerusalem.

The Roman guards forced Jesus to carry his cross all the way to that awful place. I prayed for God to help him. I hoped for a miracle. Surely, God would not allow this to happen to His own son.

---

20 Matthew 27:25 the new Open Biblke

The only help that God sent was a big strong man whom the soldiers forced to carry the cross the rest of the way. I think the soldiers only wanted the man to carry the cross because Jesus was taking so long, and they had other places they would rather be. They certainly did not care about Jesus.

I am sure Jesus would have died on the way if that man had not helped. Maybe it would have been better if that had happened. The rest was so evil I can hardly stand to think of it even now.

CHAPTER 34

GOLGOTHA

I do not know how long it took us to arrive at Golgotha. The whole thing is a blur in my mind. By the time Martha, Zilla and I got to the place, the crowd was so immense that we had to stand near the back. The place of execution was on the top of a little hill, so we could see - everyone could see - the gruesome scene.

We saw Jesus' mother, Mary, with John and Mary Magdalene near the front of the crowd. Jesus' mother was leaning heavily on John's shoulder. I felt so sorry for her. I do not know to this day how she managed to watch.

I am not going to tell all the details about the terrible torture that happened on that hill. There are many accounts of that already, and even now, it is too painful for me to think about, much less write it all down.

Jesus hung between two common thieves. The Son of God died like a criminal.

Someone had tossed Jesus' outer garments onto the ground near his cross. His beautiful robe was there, and some of the soldiers decided to help themselves to it.

They all wanted that robe, so they decided to gamble for it. About that time, I recognized

Gaius, the Roman Captain, standing near the execution site.

The solider that I had thanked for helping with my shipment of indigo was one of the men gambling for Jesus' robe. I was sorry I ever said a kind word to him. I wished he would drop dead!

He took the robe. I assumed he had won the wager. He walked over to Gaius and gave the robe to him. What was going on? Was he gamboling for Gaius? I was astounded! I was disappointed too. I had trusted Gaius, and had believed he was a friend.

The crowd was having a great time! I could not believe the things they were shouting at Jesus. Even the teachers of the law and the chief priests were shouting at him. They were saying things like, "Why don't you come down? You raised the dead, now save yourself! Why doesn't God rescue you if you are His son?"

Honestly, I was not too surprised when it began to grow dark. I thought for sure God would kill them all!

As the sky began to get dark it was more than storm clouds. It was like night coming in the middle of the day. It got pitch black.

Jesus looked down on his mother and said, "Dearest one, John will be your son now. John, she will be your mother."

Mary slumped over onto John's shoulder and wept. We all wept. From that day on, John treated Mary as if she were his own mother.

It got as dark as night. About three long hours later, we heard Jesus calling out to God. He said, "Why have you forsaken me?" I was wondering the same thing.

A soldier gave Jesus a drink, and right after that, we saw his head drop, his body sagged. We knew he was dead.

Jesus died at the exact hour when the priests sacrificed the Passover lambs. I would remember it later as proof of who Jesus really was. He was the final sacrificial lamb. We did not know it then, but it would be the last sacrifice we would ever need.

CHAPTER 35

CATASTROPHE!

All of a sudden in the darkness, the earth shook! The tremors knocked me off my feet, and many others fell down too. We were so afraid that God was going to strike us all dead!

We heard later that many people saw tombs shaken open, and dead people raised. There were other miracles also.

The heavy curtain that separated the Holy Place in the temple from the rest of the chamber tore from top to bottom. That was impossible! That curtain was so heavy that when it was time to clean it, three hundred priests were required to take the curtain down because of the weight. There were two of these curtains woven each year, so there was always one to hang when the other was in need of cleaning or repair.

When all these things started to happen, those people who were yelling, and shouting obscenities at Jesus, ran for their lives.

Our little group made our way to where John and Mary were standing. There we found Mary Magdalene, James, and many of the women from Galilee who had helped support Jesus and his disciples.

What were we going to do? We were sick with sorrow. It was nearing the Sabbath, and we were afraid that the Romans would leave Jesus' body hanging on the cross.

As we were discussing what to do, Gaius approached our little group. Oh, I wanted to spit in his face! He was carrying Jesus' robe, and he walked up to Jesus' mother Mary, and bowed at her feet.

"We wanted you to have this. My friend and I bought it from those who would have made a mockery of it. I know Jesus would have wanted you to keep it."

He handed the once beautiful robe to Mary. It was bloody, but Mary took it and wept. Gaius quietly walked away. I was astounded, and terribly ashamed of my former thoughts. I knew I would have some apologies to make later, and I prayed that I would get the chance. Mary hugged the robe close to her heart as John led her away.

We looked up and saw two men coming up toward the cross of Jesus. One was the tax collector, who had once met with Jesus and the other was with a wealthy man from Arimathea whose name was Joseph. Joseph was also a member of the ruling council. These men were coming toward the cross of Jesus. Some soldiers were with them and some servants too. The soldiers carefully removed the body of Jesus from the cross.

Nicodemus, the tax collector, had brought a huge amount of burial spices. The servants with them were carrying those spices.

As we watched, a solider took down the body of Jesus and the two men gently wrapped it, and carried it toward a garden that was not very far from the crucifixion site.

We followed along at a distance to see what they were going to do. I was very afraid, but we had to know where they were going.

When they arrived in the garden called Gethsemane, they gently laid his body down. The men wrapped it with more linen and the spices they had brought.

There was a new empty tomb there in the wall, and they placed his body inside. A huge cut stone would close the opening. It took all of the servants who had come with the men to roll the stone into place.

It was nearly dark when they left. They had hurried to finish. It was Preparation day before the Passover Sabbath, and any work had to be complete before sundown; even a burial.

We had hidden near the garden wall, and we watched all that they had done.

Now we needed to get to safety, the Passover was about to begin, and every Jew should be in their homes by this time.

Mary Magdalene was determined to come back after the Sabbaths were over. She wanted to anoint the body with oils and more spices. She was adamant about this.

We could not talk her out of it, so Mary, the mother of Jesus, her friend Salome and I made plans to come back with her after the holy days were over.

We had no idea how we were going to move that stone, but we agreed to worry about that later.

It would be two days before the Sabbaths were over, and it would be morning on the third day before we would be able see well enough to travel safely.

I hoped that the spices that the men had used would keep Jesus' body preserved until then.

Mary Magdalene had made plans to stay with the other Mary at John's house. We would meet her there after the Sabbaths.

The next day we heard that Pilate had ordered men to stand guard over the tomb. The Temple rulers had convinced Pilate that Jesus' followers might come, and try to steal his body.

Jesus had predicted that he would rise after the third day. We knew that was what Jesus had said, but I guess the horror was more than we ever imagined could happen, so we did not remember Jesus' exact words until later.

We wondered how we would be able to get into the tomb to anoint the body. Even if that huge stone rolled on a track, it would be too heavy for us to move even an inch!

Mary Magdalene said we should not worry because God would help us find a way. Oh, if we had known then what we know now! We probably would have hidden in the garden to watch no matter that it would have been against the Sabbath law.

Chapter 36

Fear and Trembling

All of Jesus' followers were keeping out of sight. Jesus' mother, Mary, was at the home of John, and the others were scattered all over the place. Martha and I barely made it home by dark.

Most of the disciples had gone back to the upstairs room where they had eaten their last meal with Jesus. No one would think to look for them there. Lazarus stayed there with them and Martha and I went to our house.

A terrible thing had happened to Judas. He must have realized what a mistake he had made by turning Jesus over to the temple leaders.

He had thought it would force Jesus to start the insurrection and declare himself King. After the arrest and trial, Judas had tried to give the bribery money back, but the leaders would not take it.

We learned that he threw the money down in front of them, and went running out of the temple.

He must have run to a place that overlooked Valley of Hinnom. There was a sort of ridge above this place, and there he hanged himself.

The weather was hot, and his body had started to decay. Because it was a Sabbath, no one would remove him from his noose. To touch a dead body on a Sabbath is against Jewish law.

The rope that he hung himself with must have broken, because his body fell over the side of the cliff and dashed to pieces below.

Vultures ate the body, and left nothing but bones. What a sad ending. If he had only waited a few more days. I know Jesus would have forgiven him for all that he had done.

Later the officials from the temple, who had bribed Judas, bought the place where his body had fallen. They used the bribery money, and made the land into a burial place for people who had no money for a tomb.

By the time we got back home that night, it was late on preparation day. The High Holy day of Passover was about to begin. We realized that our Passover lamb was still in the pen.

No one had even remembered to get him to the temple for the sacrifice. It was too late to prepare for Passover, so we prayed that God would forgive us.

We turned the lamb loose, and fed it. He later became our family pet but I am getting ahead of the story again.

Lazarus and the others were safe; we did not think anyone would come looking for a bunch of women, so we kept inside, and waited for the Sabbaths to pass. It was evening the beginning of Passover.

There were two Sabbaths that year: The Passover Sabbath, which was to start on Friday that year (starting at 6 PM and lasting until 6 PM the following day), and then our normal weekly Sabbath that began at 6 PM, and ended at 6 PM the next day.

It was actually Monday morning of the third day, three days after Jesus' death that we were able to leave home again.

Mary Magdalene, Mary the Mother of Jesus, her friend Salome, and myself, hurried along the road to the garden. We were worrying that we would not be able to roll the heavy stone away, and afraid that the guards would not let us near the tomb.

When we got there, we were shocked to see that someone had already rolled the stone away. The guards were nowhere in sight. We just knew someone had stolen his body.

We ran to the tomb, and bent down to look inside. Jesus body was not there, but a beautiful young man dressed in a bright white robe was sitting in the tomb.

This man's face glowed, and his robe was so white we almost could not look at him. We knew he must be an angel! As long as I live, I will never forget his words.

"Don't be afraid. Jesus of Nazareth who was crucified has risen! He is not here!"

"See the place where they laid him. Hurry now and go tell his disciples and Peter. Tell them that he is going to Galilee and they will see him there."[21]

We were so confused, and were still more than a little afraid. All of a sudden two more men dressed in gleaming white appeared. We knew they were angels also, and we fell on our faces in fear and awe.

"He is not here!" They said, "He has risen! Don't you remember that he told you he would die, and be raised on the third day?"

Yes! How could I have forgotten what Jesus had told us? If I had only remembered, I would not have been so terrified.

Salome, Jesus' mother and I, ran out of the tomb, and started on the way to tell the others.

In our haste and excitement, we did not notice that Mary Magdalene was not with us when we had seen the angel. We must have somehow passed her as we left and ran to tell the others.

When we finally did see her again, this is the story she told:

She had been afraid to go into the tomb at first. Then she saw us run out, and Mary feared something had happened to the body. She turned around to go for help, and saw a man

---

21 Mark 16:7

was standing there in the garden. She thought it was a gardener. She asked him if he knew who had taken the body.

Then the man spoke to her, "Mary." She said she nearly died for joy. It was Jesus! She ran to him, but he said "No, Mary. I have to go to my Father first, go find my brothers and tell them I am returning to my Father and your Father – to my God and your God. After that I will meet them in Galilee."[22]

While we were on our way to tell the disciples that the tomb was empty, Jesus appeared to us! He said, "Rejoice!"[23]

We fell at his feet and worshiped Him! I cannot even describe the joy!

Jesus told us not to be afraid, but to tell his disciples that he would meet them in Galilee.

Mary got to the upstairs room before we did. I do not know how she managed to get ahead of us. At first, the disciples did not believe her.

She later told us that Peter finally remembered what Jesus had said about coming back from the dead. They, like us, had forgotten what Jesus had told us. I guess it was so unbelievable, we really did not think he literally meant he would come back to life.

---

22 John 20:11-17 NIV

23 Matthew 28:9

The disciples all hurried back to the tomb. We met them on the way, and rushed back with them.

When they saw the tomb was empty, and we said to them again what the angels had told us, they rushed to get ready to go to Galilee.

As for the rest of us, we were so excited that we could not contain our joy. I went home, and hugged that little lamb! Lazarus came back to our house, and we spent the rest of the day praising God, and singing psalms.

The next forty days would be as nothing we had ever imagined could happen, and it all started in Galilee.

CHAPTER 37

FORTY DAYS AND FORTY NIGHTS

Jesus was true to his word and when the disciples got to Galilee, they did see Jesus. He appeared to them on several occasions there. I know that the disciples have written about their encounters with Jesus that took place over the next forty days and nights. So many miracles and joyful events took place that none of us could possibly record them all.

I was witness to so many of the wonderful things that Jesus did before he returned to God, his Father. Some of These events I witnessed myself, and some are stories that others have told.

After his resurrection, Jesus was able to walk through closed doors. More than once, he would be in one place, and disappear, only to appear somewhere else within minutes. He could appear in a room - just walk through the wall. Sometimes he would just appear out of nowhere.

Once he came to us in this way. It happened at our house. Martha, Lazarus, and I were feeding the little pet lamb. We had named him Mazalit. That name means fortunate.

All of a sudden, Jesus was there. Right in the yard by the lamb's pen. We could see all around, and there was no way he could have walked up without us being able to see him coming.

It happened a short time after he had seen his disciples in Galilee. As we talked, he explained to us that he was our sacrificial lamb. We would never have to kill another lamb to be our sin sacrifice. Just as the blood of a lamb smeared over the doors in Egypt had saved the lives of the Jew's first-born sons, Jesus' blood saved us from our sin forever!

Jesus said he had died to pay the price of our sins. We only have to believe that it is true. Jesus died at the exact time of the slaughter of the Passover lambs. He had never sinned. He was the perfect lamb.

I got it! The Messiah did not come to set us free from the Romans, but to set us free from the penalty of our sin.

We could never be perfect, but Jesus was, and he died the death that was required for the sin sacrifice for all time.

I remember saying, "But Jesus, I can't stop sinning. I try, but I always end up doing something I shouldn't."

"I know, Mary", he said, "But God accepted my perfect life as a substitute for your sin. It has been the plan since Adam first sinned. The life I lived fulfilled all the ancient prophesies.

I am the prophesied Messiah. Now all you need to do is believe that it is true, do the best you can, pray, and ask forgiveness when you mess up. I will always forgive you."

He continued, "It will not be long before I will return to heaven and to God, my father, but I will come back for all of those who believe in my sacrifice. I will take you all to be with me in heaven forever. "

At that very moment, I understood. "I want that." I said, "I believe you were my sacrifice, I get it! I watched it happen and now you are alive!'

"Mary, Martha, Lazarus, I want you to remember all these things that you have seen and tell others. I will soon go back to heaven. The eleven faithful men who have followed me will stay with me until the time when they will witness my departure from earth.

Soon after I go to be with my Father in heaven, I will send the Holy Spirit to be with you and the other believers. He will help you, and guide you in the way that you should live.

Wait for it to happen. Stay close with the others until that day.

You will know for sure when the day comes. It will be an amazing time!" Then Jesus just disappeared.

We looked at each other astounded, and finally Martha said, "Did you see that? He vanished! I do believe what he said about taking the penalty for our sin. We will all be with him again in heaven…forever!"

For 40 days, Jesus traveled around the countryside, in Galilee and in Jerusalem. Many people saw him, and several of them kept written records of many of the things that happened during that time.

He healed more people, raised some from the dead, and convinced others that he was the Messiah of whom the ancient prophets had spoken.

Many people reported seeing men and women who had been dead, walking around alive again! It was a joyful time. There had never been as happy a time on earth as those forty days.

Many of the Jews that had plotted to kill Jesus believed, and asked for his forgiveness just as we did. They became Christ followers with us.

Finally, the day came when Jesus took his closest disciples with him to a mountain, and as they watched, he rose up in a cloud, and went to the Father.

He told them to wait for the Holy Spirit to come. They came down from the mountain, and told us all about it. They were different men after that.

Those eleven men's lives were totally changed. They were no longer afraid to talk about Jesus, or afraid of the rulers. They were not afraid of anyone or anything. All they wanted to do was tell others about Jesus, and the forgiveness that could be theirs.

Peter was especially different. He had a new boldness - for Peter that was huge. He was bold before, and it nearly always got him into trouble, but now, it was almost as if telling others about Jesus was the most important thing in his life. He did not care if it was dangerous, and often it was.

These eleven men actually left their jobs, and spent all their time traveling around Judea and even as far as Greece! Many of the women that had helped Jesus when he was here traveling about, began to support his disciples as they went about telling the good news of Jesus to people all over the place.

Mary Magdalene was one of their most faithful supporters. Zilla and I helped them all too. What a joy it was to see the transformation in all our lives.

Chapter 38

A Feast I Will Never Forget

Right after the eleven followers came down from the mountain, they returned to Jerusalem with great joy. They stayed in the Temple most of the time, praising and blessing God.

Lazarus, Martha and I, along with many others, were waiting for the Holy Spirit that Jesus had promised. We often had meals together. We went to the temple every day to pray too.

Most of us stayed in Jerusalem in homes of friends who lived there. When we gathered in the temple every day, Peter told us many things about Jesus. He talked about the things Jesus had taught those men who had followed him.

The great court in the temple was huge. Many people gathered there daily to hear the disciples teach, and to pray for the One to come whom Jesus had promised to send.

Mary Magdalene, Mary the mother of Jesus, Martha, Zilla, Lazarus and myself, along with many others, met daily there. There were well over a hundred people meeting in the temple court every day.

The court was so big that many thousands could have met there, and often did, especially on feast days.

No one wanted to be too far away from the twelve disciples because we knew these men would probably be the first to see the One that Jesus had promised to send. We had no idea how awesome that gift would turn out to be.

It was nearing the time for the Feast of Pentecost, and Jerusalem was crowded with people from many cities, countries and regions. Jews from other regions, merchants, and folks who were just plain curious, had come to Jerusalem for the feast days.

The sound of so many diverse languages spoken at the same time was like listening to a babbling brook rushing down a mountainside.

The feast of First Fruits, Pentecost, is a required feast for the Jews. It is a celebration of the first fruits of the greater harvest to come. It begins at sunrise with the sacrifice of the first of the year's harvest, burning of incense, and the morning prayers.

All of us, who were waiting for the gift Jesus had promised, went to the temple to observe the feast also. After all, we were still Jews. Knowing who our Messiah is did not change that fact.

It was during the prayers that a wonderful and strange thing happened.

We often prayed aloud, and during the last prayers to God for the coming harvest, all of the Jesus followers saw what looked like the flames of many candles hovering over the heads of each of Jesus' followers.

Not only that, but we too became so courageous that we began to tell about Jesus, and how He is our Messiah.

What was so amazing was that we all were speaking in a language of a foreign nation. Languages that none of us had known before!

It was not as if we were babbling, although it actually did sound like a mighty, rushing stream.

What we soon learned was that the people visiting Jerusalem from other regions could understand every word we spoke. We were telling about Jesus in their native language. It was amazing!

Then Peter stood up, and boldly told all the people of Jerusalem exactly who Jesus was, and how his life and death fulfilled all the prophets.

Oh, many of them realized that they had called for the crucifixion of their own Messiah. They began to weep, and they asked Peter, "What can we do now?" Peter told them to repent of their sins, join us in baptism as a symbol of their repentance.

At that very moment, those people prayed to God for forgiveness.

A little later that day, all the disciples took the new believers to the pool of Salome. It is located just outside the city. There they baptized all the new believers and those people became Jesus followers too.

So many thousands became believers, and joined with us that we could not begin to count them!

It took the eleven disciples several hours to baptize all those new Jesus followers. There was a huge celebration in Jerusalem that afternoon.

CHAPTER 39

THE GOOD YEARS

Everyone probably will have heard about the great apostle Paul of Tarsus, by the time anyone will find and read this. He was responsible for teaching many of our people about Jesus.

Paul helped establish churches all over the place...even Greece. What a joyful time it was. Believers were meeting in homes and even in synagogues in some of the towns.

Do you remember the Roman soldier who had attacked me? The one I had forgiven. He became a believer. Everything about him changed.

I do not think Rome considered our movement a threat to their power, so he was not in any danger. He asked me to forgive him for that incident in my field. He actually shed tears when he begged my forgiveness. Of course, I had forgiven him several years ago, and I told him that. He became very good friends with my family, and he often visited our home.

The best news of all is about Martha. Do you remember Nathan, the boy she had hoped to marry? Nathan never married either.

He said he never found anyone he loved as much as he did Martha.

He and Martha had always been good friends, and we often saw him at social events and other places where we all gathered.

Nathan told us that he had tried to tell Martha that he would adopt Lazarus and myself, but she felt that he was only feeling sorry for her. Doesn't that sound just like Martha?

Anyway, Nathan became a believer, and he met with our little group when we worshiped together at the home of Timothy.

Timothy's father owned the house where we gathered. This was the same home where Jesus and his followers had eaten their last meal before Jesus' crucifixion.

It was no surprise to any of us when Nathan and Martha renewed their friendship. They fell in love all over again.

Lazarus and I were no longer in need of Martha's care, so a year later, Nathan and Martha were married in a small ceremony in my garden. Lazarus gave her away, and I provided a dowry of as much beautiful Indigo cloth as a wagon would hold.

Some of us have to wait a long time for God's plan to unfold. Never give up on your dreams!

For quite some time after that, we all felt relatively safe. Many of the temple leaders who had opposed Jesus had become believers, but the few that were not, were still a problem for followers of Jesus.

Lazarus was one of the people who was in danger. We found out that some of the old enemies of Jesus wanted to kill Lazarus.

Lazarus boldly told the story of his own resurrection to anyone who would sit and listen.

Many of those men and women that listened to Lazarus became Christ followers because of his testimony. This intimidated quite a few of the Jews who held office in high places.

After threats on his life, Lazarus left Judea, and went to live in Cyprus.

Countless people there became believers. Lazarus was the leader of one of the first groups of Jesus followers there. He married a sweet woman who belonged to the fellowship in Cyprus. They had three children; two boys and a girl. I am Aunt Mary now.

I love showing my flowers and the herb garden to my nephews and my sweet little niece. I tell them stories about my friend Jesus when we all sit and talk together under the Olive tree.

One of my nephew's is very interested in the indigo process. Maybe I will have someone who will carry on our business when Zilla and I are gone to our heavenly home.

Zilla never married. She said she had been married more than her share, and was perfectly able to take care of herself.

The original disciples led groups of men and women who traveled around the county teaching, making new followers, and baptizing men, women and children into the body of believers.

People began to call us Christ followers, and Jesus became known as Jesus the Christ. Christ is a Greek word that means Anointed or Chosen.

Mary Magdalene, my friend Lydia, from Thyatira, and several other women helped support Paul of Tarsus and the other disciples as they traveled from place to place spreading what we called "The Good News." It was good news for sure!

We no longer had to keep all those ridiculous rules that the Pharisees had added to God's law. We held to the written Laws of Moses, the Ten Commandments, and we trusted the Holy Spirit to guide us to do what was right and pleasing to God.

We learned how to discern when we had done something wrong, and quickly pray for God to forgive us, just as Jesus had taught us to do.

Many of the new Jesus followers met in local synagogues and in homes. We still kept the feasts of our ancestors. These feasts all reminded us of what Jesus had done for us.

Christ followers were growing in number, but the Jews still outnumbered us by vast amounts.

I believe that the Holy Spirit kept us safe during those first exciting years.

CHAPTER 40

THREATENED AGAIN

As I mentioned in the beginning of my story, our security did not last long. Roman politics were always changing, and every time a new leader took over, we had to be careful.

Jews are still under the rule of Rome. Roman kings and governors are a power-hungry bunch.

The Jewish leaders are often as power-hungry as the Romans. These Jews fear that Christians might try to overthrow the government, or try to usurp their authority. That is the last thing on any Christian's mind, but we cannot seem to convince most of the Jewish hierarchy of that truth. We are still Jews. We are just Jews who know who our Messiah is and the real reason He came.

Once again, we are living in perilous times. Jewish leaders have threatened the great teacher Paul's life, and arrested him so many times I have lost count.

So far, the women have been safe. I believe Zilla, Mary Magdalene, myself, and probably Martha, are safe from arrest because of our Indigo.

The Romans and Jews still love to flaunt their beautiful blue garments. The Romans especially, do not want to lose a source of the coveted purple cloth.

That all could change at the whim of anyone in charge of government issues, so we stay watchful.

Lydia is still helping Paul and others with expenses, and she has remained safe for the same reasons as our little group from Bethany. However, we fear that our time of security may be over soon.

The new emperor, Nero, is insane! We should not be too surprised at this. His mother was Herodias, the one who devised the plan to murder John the Baptist.

He truly is insane! He loves to burn things; buildings, homes, even people! He is one of the most deranged men I have ever heard of.

We even overheard that he is lighting his garden path with the burning bodies of people arrested for crimes against Rome. Many of those are Christ followers. I can hardly bear to think of that, much less, write it here.

For these reasons, I needed to write this account, and find a safe place to keep my story.

If you are reading this, I am probably dead. Maybe I will have lived out my life in safety, or maybe, I too, will light up Nero's garden.

All I know for sure is that no matter how I die, I will go to live forever in heaven with my Savior, friend, and Lord, Jesus the Christ. I hope I will see you there one day too.

I would love to tell you about many things that I did not have time to write here. We will have all eternity to talk together!

If you enjoyed this little book, please go to Amazon and leave an honest review. I will thank you in advance for that.

Check out my author page on the internet and sign up for my emails. I promise not to deluge your inbox with junk, but I will send you notices of sales, new books or a blog post now and then, when I think it would be of interest to you. My website is http://www.kathygreenbooks.com/

God Bless You All!
Kathy M Green

www.ingramcontent.com/pod-product-compliance
Lightning Source LLC
Chambersburg PA
CBHW070841120626
46556CB00002B/835